Steven Jordan

A Hustler's Deceit 2

Lock Down Publications & Ca$h Presents
A Hustler's Deceit 2

.

Lock Down Publications
P.O. Box 1482
Pine Lake, Ga 30072-1482

Visit our website at **www.lockdownpublications.com**

First Edition July 2017
Printed in the United States of America
This is a work of fiction. Names, characters, places, and incidents either are products of the author's imagination or are used fictitiously. Any similarity to actual events or locales or persons, living or dead, is entirely coincidental.

Cover design and layout by: Dynasty's Cover Me
Book interior design by: Shawn Walker
Edited by: Tumika Cain

Stay Connected with Us!

Text **LOCKDOWN** to 22828 to stay up-to-date with new releases, sneak peaks, contests and more…

Thank you!

Submission Guideline.

Submit the first three chapters of your completed manuscript to ldpsubmissions@gmail.com, subject line: Your book's title. The manuscript must be in a .doc file and sent as an attachment. Document should be in Times New Roman, double spaced and in size 12 font. Also, provide your synopsis and full contact information. If sending multiple submissions, they must each be in a separate email.

Have a story but no way to send it electronically? You can still submit to LDP/Ca$h Presents. Send in the first three chapters, written or typed, of your completed manuscript to:

LDP: Submissions Dept
Po Box 1482
Pine Lake, Ga 30072

DO NOT send original manuscript. Must be a duplicate.

Provide your synopsis and a cover letter containing your full contact information.

Thanks for considering LDP and Ca$h Presents.

ACKNOWLEDGEMENTS

All glory to God, because I should've been dead. I'm thankful. Shout out to my nigga, Cash, I seen the real in you from the jump. Thanks for the opportunity. And to the rest of the LDP fam I see you and appreciate the love. To everybody out there whose been ridin' with me and feeling what I'm writing, I appreciate you fucking with a real nigga. And if you ain't fucking with me or feeling my demonstration then keep that shit to yourself. I ain't the one. To all the gangstas I know clockin' numbers or still doing dirt, stay focused and far away from them fuck niggas. You know how the game go, so don't allow yourself to get played. A-town, we in this bitch!

DEDICATION

This book is dedicated to the game. I'm not saying good-bye, I'm just saying I'll see you later.

Chapter 1
2007

I could feel the heat of her stare on my back willing me to turn around and face her, but I couldn't do that just yet. Instead, I kept my eyes forward on the judge that was now stepping down from the bench, while trying to drown out the frenzied noise around me. I could tell just by the volume of the conversations going on that the spectators were filled with shock and awe at the turn of events, but I knew none were more blindsided than Carmen. On the one hand, she'd gotten what she so desperately wanted because I wasn't gonna do another day in prison, but in the same breath she'd lost another man she loved. How would she handle it?

I'd never had a doubt of whether or not my plan would work. I'd only wondered how she would handle it. I knew how strong and resilient she was, and I knew the love she had for me went deeper than any ocean. Still, I'd just sentenced her brother to certain death at the hands of the Virginia Department of Corrections, and that wasn't a "time heals all wounds" type of betrayal. My only hope was that I could get her to listen to me before she flipped the fuck out.

"You know you'll have to go back to the prison and be processed out, but it shouldn't take more than a couple of hours," my lawyer leaned over and said to me.

I nodded my head in understanding, still feeling my wife's eyes on my back and knowing I had to turn around and say something before I was snatched out of the courtroom by my escorts.

"Charles, do me a favor and buy me some time with the COs so I can have a few words with my wife. Just stall them by explaining what happens next."

Without hesitation, he got on the task at hand, which meant I couldn't put off the inevitable any longer. Taking a deep breath, I turned to find Carmen sitting stone still in the gallery, her beautiful face contorted by bewilderment as her eyes rained tears. The pain in her eyes matched her black dress, and gave off the feeling that we were standing graveside mourning together. What I needed to know was if we were mourning the loss of Rocko or us.

"Baby, I-I'm sorry. I wanted to tell you, but there wasn't enough time…"

"Zayvion, wh-what did you just do?" she asked in a strangled whisper.

How did I answer that question? There was no simple answer, and there damn sure wasn't a pretty one to make any of this easier for her to deal with. My only option was to keep shit funky.

"I did what you wanted me to do and I kept myself out of prison."

"But…but you're gonna testify against Rocko? My brother?"

"Did you miss the part where they said he was the confidential informant and he was about to hand them my black ass on a silver platter?" I asked, frustrated, trying not to lose my cool and keep my face expressionless while explaining myself.

It had been my hope that using this rationale would put shit into perspective for her, but I could tell by the fire in her eyes that two wrongs didn't make it right.

"That's my brother, Zayvion! And I don't wanna hear any bullshit about there not being enough time to tell me, because you damn sure had enough time to give the government a case against him. I could've talked him out of testifying against you if you would've just fucking told me, but you had to do it your way," she ranted in a fierce whisper. I could tell by how tightly she was clenching her purse and the look in her eyes that her pain was on another level. For a second I thought she was gonna punch me in my shit.

"Baby, listen…"

"Just shut the fuck up!" she yelled, hopping up and rushing from the courtroom. Everything in me wanted to run after her, but I knew I'd be tackled by the help before I took three good steps. Logically, I was in no position to expect Carmen's loyalty, even if she was my wife. No doubt my actions had demonstrated that I was only concerned with her title and feelings when it suited me, but her leaving still stung.

In my mind, I'd always seen this confrontation going differently, mainly because I'd planned to just pick up and leave once I was given my freedom. How could I do that now knowing Carmen was pregnant? I couldn't leave her behind with two kids on her own, no matter how much she hated me at the moment. The turmoil I was feeling would have to wait because the show had to go on. I also had to think about Iesha, the prison nurse I'd been banging, and the baby she was carrying too, because that child hadn't asked to have me for its father any more than my other ones.

When I factored in Alexis, my other sidepiece, and her 3 kids I was now a father of 6, whose life expectancy was under reconsideration depending on how the streets responded to what I'd just done. What the hell had I gotten myself into? How in the hell did I have a wife at home and two sidepieces who worked at the same correctional facility that has held me captive?

"Aight, Miller, it's time to take that ride," the CO said, taking my arm and leading me towards the courtroom exit.

I didn't resist, the quicker they got me back to the Powhatan Correctional Center the quicker I'd be released. And then what? Alexis was expecting me to come home to her so we could start our new lives together, but somehow that picture perfect image was fading with each step I took towards freedom. As I was being led to the elevator and back out into the waiting transport vehicle I took stock of the last few months of my life.

Shit had gone so wrong so fast, but I'd always known it would be like this, hadn't I? Most niggas would feel some type of way about their right-hand man, their most trusted advisor in the street game, giving up their whole operation to the feds. I didn't feel anything though, because I'd always known no one was to be trusted. The legacy of a snake tricking goes all the way back to biblical times, so whoever didn't learn to keep that grass cut deserved to be bit. One could argue that I was more of a snake than Rocko was because I'd had the presence of mind to frame him for a crime years before he ever betrayed me.

I'd take that as a compliment though because snakes ate rats. What I'd done was protect myself because I understood that only those closest to me could do the most harm. Rocko had betrayed me just because, and that was the difference between the two. Did I think I was better than him? No, but I was definitely smarter, because while he was going down for a capital murder that I committed, I would be retaking my seat on the throne. I probably should have felt bad, but what I was really feeling was relief. It had taken ruthless calculation to save myself, but because I hurt Carmen it wasn't exactly something I could be happy about. Chess wasn't a game you played for second place. You had to make moves to win at all costs. I wouldn't apologize for that. Not now, not ever.

Chapter 2
Carmen

I barely made it into the parking lot before I lost my battle with the bile rising in my throat and I vomited violently all over the asphalt. My mind swam like all of this had been a mirage in a bad dream, but I knew what the truth was because I'd witnessed it. The shock of seeing my big brother being led into the courtroom to testify against my own husband had stopped my heart in my chest, but the way Zayvion turned the tables on Rocko made me think my heart wouldn't beat again! How could they do that to each other? How the fuck could they do that to me! Both of them knew the code of the streets and they'd always played by the rules, so to see all that loyalty vanish in the blink of an eye was something I couldn't understand.

"Are you alright, ma'am?" a Sheriff's deputy asked, stopping beside me.

"I'm fine," I replied, wiping my mouth and hurrying to my silver 2006 BMW M3.

It took me four tries to get the damn key in the lock before I could open the door and throw myself inside. I felt like the world was watching me, like everyone was enjoying the show and spectacle of my family crumbling under the law's pressure. I may not have been as entrenched as Zay or Rocko in the streets, but I would still be judged, and so would my kids.

"Oh God," I said, my hands going to my stomach as I leaned my head back against my seat and shut my eyes.

The tears wouldn't stop pouring, but now they were coming for different reasons. I hadn't been able to deny the fear I'd felt when I learned I was pregnant, because Zayvion's future had been so uncertain, but I was still happy because I wanted another child with him. At the moment, I didn't know how I'd ever look him in the eye again knowing that he'd just killed my only brother. In my mind, I understood the kill or be killed mentality, but the heartache of what was really going on right now made logical thought impossible.

There were so many questions I needed answers to in order to diffuse the warring emotions inside me! My anger at both Rocko and Zay was fighting for dominance, but my utter confusion about everything didn't allow my emotions a clear path. Why had Rocko snitched on Zay? What had really been going on between them right under my nose, and how the fuck had I missed it? Niggas didn't just wake up one day and decide to fuck over their right-hand man, and even though there was no justification for what either of them did, there still had to be a reason. Before I could make a decision, I had to know exactly what was going on. My come to Jesus conversations with Zay would happen soon enough since he was miraculously a free man, so for now I'd start with my brother.

As much as I didn't wanna walk back into that courthouse I knew I had to. There was no telling where the feds were taking Rocko, but I knew he had to still be somewhere in the building. Taking several deep breaths, I grabbed my purse from the passenger seat where I'd flung it and stepped back out of my car. It made sense to hide my eyes behind my big sunglasses, because the world didn't deserve an in depth look at my devastation. Head held high, I walked briskly back into the building and straight to the clerk's desk where a young Spanish chic was filing her nails.

"Excuse me, I need to know where my brother, Raymond Vargas, is being held in this building."

I expected stank attitude because I was obviously interrupting her leisure time, and if she took it there I was gonna get on that ass. Instead, she put her nail file to the side and started hitting keys on the computer keyboard.

"Did he have a court case this morning?" she asked.

"Something like that. H-he was supposed to testify in the Zayvion Miller case."

"Oh…well that case's deposition hasn't been entered into the computer yet, so he might still be inside the courtroom or…"

"You don't understand, my brother was arrested and he's now facing a case. All of this shit just happened a few minutes ago, which means my brother is somewhere in this damn building, and I wanna see him," I said forcefully.

When her eyes snapped up and met mine I could see the attitude clearly, but I was down to twist a bitch's wig without hesitation if she uttered a wrong word. Even behind my shades my eyes must've conveyed this message because home girl checked her attitude and reached for the phone on her desk. I listened closely as she ran down my situation to whoever was on the other end, but their response was so short that I thought she'd been told to dismiss me.

"Someone will be with you momentarily," she said, picking her nail file back up and going back to the task at hand.

The anger I was feeling wasn't really meant for her, but at this point anyone in my path could get it. Right now, I was down to inflict pain on anyone, because the shit I was feeling was too much to carry alone.

"Mrs. Vargas?" a woman said stopping in front of me.

I recognized her slim build, blue pantsuit, and Afrocentric blowout from the courtroom. She was the District Attorney.

"My name is..."

"I know who you are, Mrs. Watkins. Where is my brother?" I asked, all business.

Truthfully, I wanted to get on her mufuckin' helmet and rock her fast and hard, but then I'd surely be giving birth behind bars. This bitch was a facilitator in my brother and husband turning on each other, and it was a damn shame, because as a black woman she should understand that prisons were already overly populated with our men. Now wasn't the time for me to run this down to her though, because it was obvious I needed her to get to Rocko.

"You can only have a few minutes with your brother, because he's getting ready to be extradited. Follow me."

"Extradited where?" I asked, falling into step beside her as we navigated the busy halls of the courthouse.

"The capital murder charge he's facing is in northern Virginia, Fairfax County to be exact, so he has to be transported back up there."

"Will he be given a bond?" I asked, hopeful.

I noticed she cut her eyes in my direction before she answered, undoubtedly sizing me up to see if I could handle the truth. Like a lie was gonna do me any goddamn good at this point!

"With a crime this serious, I highly doubt it, but I can't say for sure, because it's a state matter for the moment. You've got 10 minutes," she said stopping in front of a solid oak door. It was opened immediately by a huge white dude with close cut blonde hair, and a shirt that was 3 sizes too small. Steroids had done the body good.

"You can wait outside," she told him.

When he stepped aside I was given a clear view of Rocko sitting in handcuffs at the far side of a cheap wooden table. The sister in me wanted to run to him the same way I had as a little girl when I was scared, but the wife and mother in me wanted answers more than a hug. For the first time in my memory Rocko looked smaller than his 6'4, 270 pound frame that easily intimidated most mufuckas. He had a quick smile that masked the intelligence behind his dark brown eyes, but at the moment his face was a mask of uncertainty.

From personal experience, I knew my brother didn't fear nothing or no one, but I could tell even he was smart enough to see how fucked up this was. His light brown skin looked a little pale and I could tell it was an effort to keep his poker face intact. But once the door closed behind me and we were alone I saw his guard slip a little. There was only one other chair in the windowless room, but I stood behind it instead of sitting across from him. The restless shift of his eyes touching everything in the room except me spoke of his guilt, but I only wanted to know one thing.

"Why, bruh? Why would you turn on my husband, your best friend, and try to get him put under the jail?"

"Ain't it obvious that he would've done the same to me if he was in my situation?"

"What situation? You were running around free as a bird while he was serving his violation time! You had no fucking reason to try and bury him!" I raged, tears once again clouding my vision.

"I got caught up," he mumbled weakly.

"What the fuck are you talking about?"

"I made a bad deal without consulting Zay and it turned out to be the feds. They had enough to put my black ass away forever if I didn't agree to give up my connect, so I did what I had to do."

"But Zayvion ain't your connect he..."

"I know what he is and what he ain't, and this ain't a conversation we need to be having in a federal courthouse," he interjected quickly.

The look he was giving me was one I understood, because no one knew my brother like I did. There walls had ears, but more importantly than that was the understanding that Rocko could never give up their real connection to the dope and guns. To do that would mean certain death for everyone, my daughter included. That still didn't justify his decision to serve up my daughter's father to the fucking feds though.

"There had to have been another way, Rocko. You and Zay been through too much together to..."

"Yeah, we been through so much that this nigga had a plan more than 5 years in the making to set me up," he said, giving me a sad smile.

I opened my mouth to speak, but was forced to quickly shut it as I thought about what I'd heard in the courtroom earlier. Zayvion's testimony wasn't about a recent murder. It was about an unsolved cold case, and 5 years ago, was when he'd gotten out after doing that year. He'd said he'd had an insurance plan to keep him out of prison, but there was no way he meant...

"I-I don't understand," I stammered.

"Yes, you do. I can see it in your eyes. You ain't no dummy, Carmen. I admit that, but that was only after I got jammed up and you know why I couldn't give them what they wanted. Dude has been plotting on me for years though."

"Why? What went so wrong between you two?" I asked, hoping for some type of clarity.

Rocko was silent for a while, almost like he was searching for the answer to that question his damn self.

"Money and friendship don't mix, because no matter how much money you make it's never enough to feed that animal called greed. For years I ain't been getting what I deserved, which was why I started making my own moves and my own deals."

"And thinking about yourself, huh? Did me or your niece ever cross your mind before you decided to destroy this family? What about the baby I'm carrying now? Oh, you looked surprised, I forgot to tell you the good news about me being pregnant. You don't give a fuck though, right? It's all about that almighty dollar," I said, hating the fact that I couldn't stop the tears or the raw emotions pouring out of me.

"There's nothing I can say that makes this better, Carmen, and apologizing would be spitting in your face. Did I fuck up? Yes, but I didn't do this."

"What do you mean?" I asked, swiping at my tears and looking at him closely.

"Come on, sis, you know me. I'm a lot of things, and that may hypothetically include being a killer if someone came for me, but when have you ever known me to do some reckless shit like kill a cop?"

My brother was a true street nigga, or at least I'd always thought so, and I knew he'd never openly admit to knocking a cop off. His eyes were speaking truth to me though.

"So, what are you saying, Rocko?" I asked.

"I'm saying I don't think either of us knows Zayvion for real, because if he thought this far ahead to set me up, what else is he capable of? If I can't trust him, do you think you can?"

Chapter 3
Rocko

The door opening behind her stopped whatever answer she was about to give, but I could see the uncertainty in her eyes.

"Time's up, miss. We gotta move him now," the big cop with the too tight t-shirt informed us.

I hated to see Carmen cry, especially because I knew it was my fault, but I knew there was nothing I could do about it. I'd played my hand the way I thought I had to, and now I had to deal with the consequences.

"Call me as soon as you get to the jail," she said.

"I will. Stay away from him, Carmen. Just take Ariel and go someplace safe."

Even though she nodded her head in acknowledgement of what I said, I knew she probably wouldn't listen. Love was truly blind at times, and I knew now better than ever that Zay had us both fooled. It hurt to watch my baby sister walk away from me, and for the first time in my 27 years I wondered if I'd ever see her again. She was right to be angry with me, or even hate me for what I'd tried to do, but in my heart, I was holding on to the hope that our bond could survive this. Carmen was all I had in this world and I never wanted to lose that.

Before our defection from Cuba I had promised our parents that I would always take care of her, but for the first time I felt like a complete fucking failure. Time and time again I'd rationalized the decision to give up Zayvion in my mind as something that had to be done because telling on our real connect wasn't a possibility. Their reach was too long, and women and children were fair game to make examples out of. Self-preservation had forced me to violate the street code, but it had also been about protecting my sister. Maybe one day she would see that, if she could ever see past Zayvion and his bullshit.

"Stand up, Vargas, we've got some accessories to go with your nice blue suit," a short, bald cop ordered, coming into the tiny room.

I did as I was told, smoothing the wrinkles out of my tailored Tom Ford suit while the cop stepped forward and fitted me with a waist chain and black box to go with the handcuffs already on my wrist. To be honest, I hadn't been looking forward to this day in court for a few reasons, and I'd seen it going a lot of different ways, but not like this. It was still hard to comprehend how the hell I was now being transported to a county jail to face a crime I didn't commit. It was almost too crazy to believe. Almost.

"How long is it gonna take to get where we're going?" I asked.

"One thing you shouldn't stress yourself with is time, because as far as you're concerned it's lost all meaning for you," the big cop said with a smile.

My smartass remark was on the tip of my tongue, but the tightening of my handcuffs let me know it wasn't a good idea. I was led from the room by my two escorts and into a stairwell that took us two floors down into a dimly lit parking garage. An all-black unmarked '07 Dodge Challenger awaited me as soon as I stepped out of the stairwell, and I was shoved into the backseat with the delicacy reserved for cop killers.

"Let's go, Erica," the big cop said to the strawberry blonde chic behind the wheel.

Our eyes met briefly in the rearview mirror and I was pulled in by the pale blue in hers, but the disgust she felt was obvious and instantaneous. It didn't matter though, because where I was headed, the affections of a female were the least of my concerns. What I needed to figure out was how the fuck Zay had boxed me in like this. Killing a cop was something hard to forget, so I was positive I hadn't actually pulled the trigger. My prints were on the gun though.

Zay and I shared a lot of things, but not guns, and I knew damn well the police didn't have any gun that belonged to me, because I didn't hold on to dirty shit. Getting my prints on one of his guns would've been easy for Zay though, I mean I wouldn't have ever suspected he was trying to frame me. A move like this took extreme patience and calculation, both of which I didn't give that nigga credit for having. I never thought he was a dummy, because I never could've rocked with him for all those years, but I damn sure didn't think he was an evil genius.

Five years he'd been laying low and waiting, lurking, smiling in my face while making sure the knife he had lined up for my back would sever my spine. How the fuck had I missed that? Had I been so focused on making more money than him that I forgot how ruthless this game truly was? I never considered myself so dumb as to trust a nigga, but it seemed like I'd made the bigger mistake of underestimating one. In all the years, we'd known each other we'd had few occasions to argue and no real cause to fall out. It was because of that I could keep my own treachery a secret until the actual day I had to testify.

Now as I was being whisked away to an unsure future I was left wondering if my own deceit had blinded me to his. The more pressing question was what my next move would be. It was gonna take an entire legal team to get from under this case, but this is what niggas in the game saved money for. Given the nature of the crime and my priors I probably wouldn't get a bond, but county time wasn't shit to cry about.

Tuning out the voices of the cops, the squawking of their radios, and the world moving past me outside the car windows, I got down to the business of planning my next moves. I had no doubt or illusions that Zayvion's first act of business would be to turn the streets against me and take everything for himself. You'd think that would be impossible given the fact that he was now set to testify against me, but the difference in our sins was that he'd betrayed me, while I'd betrayed the game. One could be forgiven or maybe even celebrated, but the other meant I was now a pariah.

The only person I could count on was my girl, and I had to keep her out of harm's way, because Zay would definitely eliminate her out of spite. The person I truly needed in this moment was Carmen, because I doubted anyone else could keep her rabid dog on his leash. I had to plan and plot like she wasn't on my team. The pain of just thinking that was unbearable and I forced myself to lock it away, because now wasn't the time to drown. I don't know how much time passed, but before I knew it we were pulling into the parking garage beneath the Fairfax County Adult Detention Center. On more than one occasion I'd been a guest of this particular roach motel, and I didn't relish the thought of being back.

"Welcome to your new home, Vargas," the big cop said, earning him a slight snicker from his female counterpart as she put the car in park.

"Do they still offer turn down service?" I asked, locking eyes with the female cop in the rearview mirror again. It didn't pay to be a smartass, but the dislike between us was understood and mutual just based on the looks we exchanged.

"Oh, I'm sure they'll roll out the welcome mat for you, don't you worry," she said, flashing me a smile that never quite reached her eyes.

Once they both got out and stored their weapons I was pulled from the car and pushed in through the doors that led to booking.

"Looks like we got a fancy one here," the short, fat cop sitting behind the booking desk commented.

"Don't let the suit fool you, Jimmy, this one here is a killer," the big cop replied, pushing me up against the desk.

"You don't say? Well, who'd you kill?"

"I didn't kill nobody. I…"

"Paul Blankenship."

Those two words spoken by the petite cop, Erica, were enough to stop all movement and bring a hush over the room. I could feel every set of eyes turn in my direction, and the feeling in the pit of my stomach told me it wasn't admiration in those looks.

"You're the one who killed Paul?" Jimmy the desk sergeant asked calmly.

This whole situation felt like an old western and I was damn near expecting to hear some type of eerie theme music start to play in the background.

"I didn't kill nobody, I'm being set up." Even to my own ears my protests sounded weak, but that didn't make them any less true.

"Innocent 'til proven guilty, huh?" Jimmy asked.

"Not around here," someone behind me said.

"Look, man, I don't owe none of you no explanation, so let's get this show on the road so I can get my bag lunch and a nap," I said, tired of playing games with these mufuckas.

"Thanks for bringing him in, Frank, we can handle it from here," Jimmy said, smiling in an unsettling way and giving the big cop next to me a little salute.

I heard the laugh as he backed away from me and re- traced his steps, with his partner in tow, and I knew it was gonna be a long night. All at once everyone got back to the business of doing their jobs, and Jimmy came from around the desk to unhook me from all the heavy metal. It took about an hour to get my prints and pictures done, but since I had plenty of time on my hands, I wasn't trippin.' Finally, the time came for me to change out of my clothes and into their shit green jumpsuit before I could make my first phone call.

Jimmy led me to the changing room and passed me my clothes, but before I could undress five cops in all black standing at least 6'3 or better and weighing in the mid 200s filed in. There was no doubt in my mind what this was, but at least they'd given me the courtesy of not being handcuffed for it. As soon as Jimmy backed his short, fat ass out the door I grabbed the closest one to me and head-butted him with the force of a charging bull. My vision swam briefly, but I was already firing jabs at the next man in line because offense was my only defense.

When the second one dropped, I thought I had a shot at victory, and then I felt the storm of 50,000 volts hit me harder than any man ever had. In my mind, I was scream- ing "don't go down," but, I was already on my back looking up at the boots raining fury on my body. I tried to curl up and protect myself, but that only earned me anoth- er jolt of lightening from the Taser. There was nothing I could do except take what they were so eager to give.

When their boots found my nuts, I threw up, and by the time they reached my face I was thankful to blackout.

Chapter 4
Zay

"Uh-uh, don't run. This is what you been wanting right? Right?" I growled, fucking her harder.

"Yes! God yes!"

I had her bent over the sink with her face pressed up against the dingy mirror as I pulled her by the hair while drilling my dick into her. Without missing a stroke, I kicked her legs further apart and really stepped into the pussy, forcing her up on her tiptoes.

"I-I'm…I'm..."

"Cum on this dick!" I demanded, continuing my onslaught of punishing strokes as the skies between her legs opened and her delicious juices rained on me. She bucked violently beneath me, but I held on tight and gave her what I knew she wanted.

"You had enough?"

"No, no, don't s-stop," she begged.

I didn't stop, but I slowed my strokes down so she could get the complete feel of this long dick all the way in her stomach. The feeling of her pussy spasming and clinching my dick had me at the edge, but it wasn't until the walkie talkie announced that count was clear did I pick the pace back up and take us to the lands of far away. Only when I finally finished cumming did I let her down off the sink so she could turn around and face me, the look in her eyes was one of hunger and surprise, but more than anything I saw satisfaction.

"I always thought you had some good dick, but damn boy, I had no idea," Burnette panted, trying to catch her breath.

"Shit, you surprised me too. I knew you had a nice body and you're definitely beautiful, but I didn't think you could take that rough ride."

"Baby, I may not act my age or look it, but in 50 years I've had it put on me a time or two. Nothing like that though. Shit, the last mufucka who grabbed my hair I tried to cut his ass, but you could've pulled it out at the roots and I wouldn't have cared!"

"Your ass is crazy," I replied laughing, and getting myself together.

"Hold up," she said, grabbing my hand and stopping me from tucking my dick back inside my boxers. Slowly, deliberately, she ran her index finger across the head of my dick, smearing it with cum before sticking it in her mouth. "Mmm, you taste good too."

I thought she was bending down to pull her pants and panties back up until suddenly I felt the heat of her mouth engulf me.

"Bur-Burnette, you gotta open-open the doors," I said, taking her head in my hands and pushing my dick deeper down her throat.

Despite the fact that I'd just climaxed I could feel myself stirring under her expert mouth game, and if she got this mufucka back up then she was gonna get it back down. She grabbed ahold of my shaft with both hands and pulled her soft, succulent lips all the way back until she only had the head in her mouth. The way she sucked me had my knees rattling as I looked down into her sapphire blue eyes, and just as it became too much to handle she backed away.

"Damn, is your head game like that?" I asked, reluctantly letting her go.

"If you wanna know you can always come by my place tonight."

My first thought was an immediate dismissal because I had way more important shit to do and more pussy waiting on me, but given everything that had happened today it might not be a bad idea to hold up where no one knew me. During my whole ride back to the prison I'd been trying to figure out what my first move would be, but I couldn't see past Carmen. I wanted to fix the hurt and devastation I caused, but how? We couldn't unwring the bells we'd rung, and it was too soon to ask for forgiveness.

I knew she needed time, and I needed to distract myself so I wouldn't push her before she was ready to hear me. Which partially explained how I'd ended up in the staff bathroom with CO Burnette. It just so happened that I got back during count and since she was my floor officer she volunteered to escort me back upstairs. We'd always been cool so I didn't have a problem telling her that I was being released sometime today, and she didn't have a problem telling me that she'd been wanting to give me some pussy, but I acted like I was scared of it. Now she knew better.

"Where do you live, Burnette?"

"I live in Richmond, and I think you've earned the right to call me Nancy now," she replied, fixing her uniform.

"Okay, Nancy, you live alone?"

"Of course, sweetheart, no old man or kids to tie me down. But you can tie me up if you want to," she replied with a devilish smile.

It would seem that I had an old freak on my hands, but I also might have an opportunity to stay off the radar and get a feel for the streets before returning to Northern Virginia.

"Aight listen, I need all your info before they call me downstairs to process me out and I'll hit you up later."

"Don't bullshit either, Zayvion. I wanna see you when I get off tonight," she replied, pulling me towards her.

"Listen, Ima be real with you, it's gonna be some shit in the streets because I'm home and I really need somewhere to kick it for a few days where nobody knows me, if you cool with me hiding out at your spot then you ain't gotta worry, because Ima be there as soon as I get a few things situated."

"As long as don't no drama come to my door we're good. I'll keep you fed and put this pussy on you right," she said, squeezing my dick through my jumpsuit.

"Don't start, you know you gotta open these doors before niggas start kickin' and screaming."

Reluctantly, she stepped back and opened the bathroom door so she could peek out to make sure the coast was clear. Once she was satisfied, she signaled me and I duck walked out the bathroom, through the control room, and out into the hallway. I stayed in the shadows while she turned the knobs to open all the doors on the floor and let the other inmates out of their cells. It didn't really affect me if niggas knew I'd just finished knocking Burnette off, but I wasn't trying to get her fired because of some hating shit.

After a few minutes passed, she gave me the signal and I appeared like I'd just come out of the stairway. To her credit, she played it cool and buzzed me through the gate with nothing more than a smile. I stepped on the floor as nonchalant as I could, wanting to give the impression that this was just another day in the land of bullshit.

Only the closest niggas I fucked with knew I was going to court, although none of them had a clue about the move I had pulled to earn my freedom. In my opinion, none of them would understand, because it took a chess master to see the board as I did.

Even as I was preparing mentally to step back into my old life, I knew Rocko was trying to figure out how he never saw this coming. The lesson in the madness was to never underestimate your opponent, but before you could grasp the concept you have to understand who your opponent is. Everyone. For years, I'd let him think he was the smartest person in the room because I knew his vision was clouded by dollar signs. Money is more addicting than any drug, and I'd known Rocko was a fiend years ago, which meant I couldn't trust him. All it took for me to see that was doing that first year in county, because the streets talk. I heard the whispers. I was counting days and he'd been getting high on money and power. Bet his ass was sober now!

"What up, Zay?" Fred asked, coming towards me.

As much as I wanted out of prison it was certain dudes I was gonna miss, and my young nigga Fred was one of them. Killer or not, he was still a good dude and he didn't deserve the 64 years he was serving.

"Round up everybody and meet me in my cell," I told him, going in that direction. When I got to my door, my cousin Ham was just getting ready to come out, but I pushed him back inside.

"Damn, you back already, nigga?" he asked surprised. My response was a big ass smile from ear to ear.

"You beat it? Say something, nigga!" he said, pinching me playfully in the chest.

"Ima tell you what the deal is, just wait on everybody to get here. And roll a blunt really quick."

When he was doing that, I closed the door real quick so I could get my cell phone out of its hiding spot because I had a lot to do before I actually hit the streets.

"Open up, nigga," Boo Gotti said, banging on the door.

When I let him in he was followed by his homie Double Oh, and Fred completed the small circle of niggas I fucked with.

"Cover the window 'cause we 'bout to blow one," I said.

"Are we celebrating or nah?" Fred asked.

"Yeah, fuck all the dramatic shit, nigga, just tell us what it is," Ham said, putting the finishing touches on the blunt.

"Aight, well I ain't got time to give you mufuckas a play by play anyway, so long story short, they should be letting me out this bitch in a minute."

As soon as I revealed the news, I was mobbed by everybody in the room. Clumsy hugs were given along with playful gut punches, but I could tell that everybody was genuinely happy for me. The blunt was lit and passed around, and before it was even halfway smoked, three more had been rolled and put in rotation. I was definitely going out with a bang.

"So, how'd you pull it off?" Double Oh asked.

"Their case fell apart once my lawyer got on the witness's credibility. 50 Cent said it best, you shouldn't throw stones if you live in a glass house."

"So now what're you gonna do, because you know they gonna be watching you once you're out," Boo Gotti said.

36

"Yeah, I know, but with the kinda money we making in here I can give myself the time needed for the streets to cool down a little."

"So, what's the play?" Fred asked.

"Everything remains the same, my nigga, all you gotta do is get to the money. I'll have the first shipment here within 48 hours, that's my word."

Everyone nodded their head in agreement and we kept smoking. Once the weed was gone, I dapped everybody up and asked them to slide, so I could get right with my cousin really quick. Me and him were more like brothers, and he'd been quiet, so I knew he had some heavy shit on his mind.

"Talk to me, cuzzo," I said once we had the cell to ourselves.

"I'm good, bruh, just faded."

"I know you faded, nigga, but I know it's more than that too. So, what's up?" For a minute, he simply looked at me like he was unsure of what to say or how to say it.

"That was some serious shit you went to court for, my nigga. Shit like that ain't easy to get from up under."

"So, what are you saying?" I asked.

"I ain't saying nothing, I'm just worried about you that's all."

"I'm good and I'll be even better once they let me out this mufucka."

"Yeah, I feel that. Make sure you stay safe out there though, because it's bound to be some nigga who ain't happy to see you," he warned.

"I got a spot to rest easy at. All I want you worried about is making this money though, because it's gonna be all on you now, bruh. Can you handle it?"

"You must be high if you asking me dumb ass questions like that!" he replied laughing.

"Aight, well you know I ain't taking shit with me, so everything is yours and…"

"Miller!" Burnette hollered from the door. I turned around and opened it so she could step in. "It's time," she said, slipping a piece of paper into my hand.

"Damn already?" I asked, surprised that my reinstatement paperwork had gone through so fast.

"Are you seriously complaining?" she said laughing.

"Hell nah!"

I tucked her information in my pocket and turned back to my cousin to give him one last hug, passing him the cellphone at the same time.

"You know where everything is, I love you, bruh," I told him.

"Love you too, be safe out there and keep your eyes open."

"Don't worry I'll take care of him," Burnette whispered, making my cousin laugh and look at me with a question in his eyes.

"Don't judge me, nigga," I said, walking out the cell behind Burnette.

"Y'all hold it down in this mufucka and keep your heads up!" I yelled.

A lot of people were surprised and confused as to what was going on, but those who knew shouted at me as I made my way off the floor for the last time.

"See you later?" Burnette asked once we were on the other side of the gate.

"It might be late, because I've got business to handle, but I'll be around."

"You better be," she said, giving me a quick peck on the lips once we were out of everyone's sight.

Making my way downstairs I tried to shake the fog of the weed from my mind so I could concentrate on what I had to do next. I'd thought for sure it would take some time to get me released, but apparently, my lawyer was worth every cent I paid him. Within a half hour I was dressed in an ugly khaki uniform and walking out of the front gates with my prison I.D. and a check for $518 in my pocket. The CO at the gate told me there was a bank about a mile off the farm, so that was my destination on foot since I didn't have a ride. I'd just started up the road when she pulled up next to me and lowered the window.

"Get in the car, Zay."

I couldn't see her eyes behind her sunglasses, but I saw the cocked pistol in her lap.

Aryanna

Chapter 5
Carmen

"Don't bitch up now, nigga. Get in the fucking car," I told him. His hesitation was a clear indication of his uncertainty about what I was planning to do, and the truth was that I didn't know. I was mad enough to shoot him in his ass if he didn't get the fuck in so we could get the hell off state property. He was slow about opening the door and easing into the seat, but as soon as he did I hit the gas and squealed away. I'd lost track of how many nights I'd laid in bed fantasizing about his freedom, about having my family back, and putting all the bullshit behind us. Now it seemed like the bullshit was just getting started.

"Baby, I..."

"Don't talk until I tell you to," I said with as much calm as I could.

Truthfully, I wanted to scream on some hysterical type shit and backhand him with the butt of my Taurus 9mm, but I maintained my composure. He was smart enough to shut the fuck up too. I knew Zayvion wasn't no bitch, and yeah, he did wear the pants in our relationship, but right now he could get it like any other nigga on the street. When I'd left my brother, I'd had every intention of doing what he'd asked and staying far away from Zayvion Miller, but that would've been too easy to let him off like that. There was no way he could do the shit he just did and walk away without consequence, not to my brother.

"Rocko is my brother, Zay, My brother! Before there was ever a me and you, he was the one who took care of me. We left Cuba as kids and he's taken care of me every step of the way. You knew that, so how the fuck could you do this to him?"

"He was gonna testify…"

"Zayvion, you gave him up on a cold case! This has been your insurance plan all along, so don't come at me with no bullshit about what he was gonna do to you!"

"Are you gonna let me fucking talk or not?" he asked hotly.

I felt my hand tighten on the pistols grip involuntarily, but I still managed to hold it together enough to nodding my head so I could hear whatever bullshit excuse he was kickin'.

"You're right, I did set this in a motion a long time ago, and I'm not saying that the situation ain't fucked up, because it is. Survival in the streets is based on your ability to see what's coming, because something is always coming. Niggas want your money, your product, and the real estate you control. While bitches are looking for a come up, a sponsor, or a new baby daddy. It's the jungle, and you don't walk through the mud without being covered in slime."

"Tell me something I don't know," I said immediately.

"What you don't know is that I did what I did for you, and before you say shit just shut up and listen. You think because I'm a street nigga who understands the consequences of my decisions that doing a bid is no big deal. The truth is, that first year I had to do hurt like a mufucka because I saw how bad it devastated you. I saw you suffering every time you had to leave me after visitation. I listened to you cry because you missed me, and it broke my heart. I spent those first 6 months vowing to change and be a better man for you once I was out, and I was even willing to go straight, which was why I got my G.E.D. but a leopard can't change his spots, babe. I am the streets. So, if I couldn't change, and I was unwilling to ever be separated from you again then I had to move smarter than ever before."

"But why Rocko, Zay? You could've chose anyone else, hell one of your real enemies!"

"Because your biggest enemy is most likely the closest person to you, Carmen. Just because I was doing time in county didn't mean my ears weren't to the streets, my streets. While you were crying and I was away your brother was running around like he owned the mufuckin' world! It wasn't about what we'd built and risked our lives for. It wasn't about taking care of you like a big brother should. It was all about Rocko. If I'd been gone any longer, that nigga would've staged a complete takeover, and that would've left us with what? We deal with the cartel, Carmen, so if they would've thought me weak enough I'da been forced out of my own operation. How long do you think it would've taken to kill me? Or you? You're right, I could've chosen someone else, but the fox was in the hen house and I'd be a damn fool to let him stay there."

My anger and hurt didn't allow for reasoning…but my love for him did. As I navigated the highway before us, I weighed his words carefully against what Rocko had said earlier, and it sounded like my brother hadn't moved as stealthily as he'd thought. Zayvion was nobody's fool and he was definitely a survivor. Being immigrants had made it hard on Rocko and I, but at least we'd had the good fortune of a good aunt and uncle to take us in until the streets called. Zay had a heroin junky for a mother and a drunk for a father who loved to beat the closest person to him. While we were learning English, he'd been training in survival. Even though I knew that, and I'd always respected that, I still couldn't quite process the fact that he'd done what he did.

"Where are we going?" he asked.

When I'd decided to pick him up from prison my initial plan was to find a hole for him to eternally rest, but there was only one problem. I still fucking loved him.

"Carmen?"

"I don't know, Zayvion, just let me think for a minute. Damn!"

Thankfully, he fell silent and I kept driving north. After the shock had worn off this morning, I'd felt about a 70% need to kill him, but now that I was in his presence it was down to about 50/50. I loved my brother dearly and he had my loyalty, but what about Ariel and the baby on the way? How would I ever explain to them my decision to kill their father? And even if I never told them, how would I make up for robbing them of such a precious part of their life? My own memories of my father were fleeting and he'd died in Cuba before I could ever think about going back.

Did I really wanna rob my kids of their dad? I'd been navigating the car with my left hand. Because my gun was still in my right, but I didn't flinch when he put his hand on top of mine and gently rubbed the back of it. I didn't release my grip on the pistol, but I didn't tell him to stop either. The truth is that I missed this man's touch more than anything in the world. Too many nights I'd spent at home holding myself or trying to draw comfort from a 3-year-old who was a mirror image of the man next to me.

Ariel may have looked like me, but she was her father's daughter 100%. For a while we continued riding in silence, seemingly a world apart, even though we were only a breath away from each other. Zayvion was a man of power and I could feel that power even though it was firmly harnessed by his patience. God help me, but I loved this man! I gently lifted his hand off of mine, uncocked the pistol, and laid it in the center console before retaking his hand.

"I'm sorry, baby," he said, lacing our fingers together and squeezing my hand in comfort.

I didn't trust my voice, so I didn't say anything. I just kept driving and praying I'd be able to see through my tears. Part of me felt like I was betraying my brother, and I had no idea how to deal with that because he'd always been there for me. I had to figure out a way to be there for him, because I couldn't choose between him and Zay. I just couldn't.

"I need to ask you something, Zay, and please don't lie to me," I said. He didn't say anything, but I felt him staring at me. "Before I came to pick you up I went and saw Rocko. He admitted that his greed had gotten the better of him, and that he'd made a bad business decision that brought him face to face with the feds. The only deal they'd given him was if-if he'd give up the connect, but he said…"

"That he couldn't do that because they'd kill everybody," he interjected.

"Yeah. I'm not telling you this to try and excuse what he did, I'm telling you because based on what he said it sounds like the truth. He also told me that he didn't kill no cop," I said, glancing at him out of the corner of my eye to catch his reaction. Unsurprisingly, his poker face stayed intact.

"What's your question, Carmen?"

"I think you know what my question is...did my brother kill that cop or did you frame him for the whole thing?"

When he let my hand go I thought he might've been reaching for my gun, but instead he turned in his seat to face me while using his other hand to take my glasses off.

"Baby, what was he supposed to say to you? I know how much you love him, and I wish shit wasn't the way it is, but you know I didn't frame him. He made a move he felt like he had to make, and it was sloppy. You may think I'm a piece of shit for capitalizing off his mistake, but at the end of the day it's still his mistake."

I'd known Zay long enough to see through his bullshit and right now I could see how sincere he was being. Deep down I'd known it was a possibility that Rocko hadn't wanted to disappoint me, not to mention the fact that our conversations were undoubtedly being listened to. His guilt or innocence didn't change the fact that he was my brother and I loved him, and no matter how much I loved Zay I couldn't leave Rocko for dead.

"So, what happens now?" I asked.

"What do you mean?"

"I mean the streets ain't forgiving, Zay, and neither are your business associates. This shit ain't gonna go over well when word gets out."

"Ima handle it, don't worry," he replied, taking my hand again.

"I'm not just talking about protecting me and the kids, or smoothing shit over so you can continue to do what you do. You gotta fix this."

"Fix it how?"

"I don't know, but if you love me like you say you do you'll figure it out. You know like I do what capital murder carries, Zay. Please. Please don't let them kill my brother."

Chapter 6
Rocko

I'd always thought that being unconscious would be some kind of dreamlike state where you saw flashes of the past or maybe even hopes for the future, but it wasn't like that. You were simply suspended in darkness until all of a sudden you weren't. I remember the flurry of boots coming towards my face and head, and the pain that accompanied them, and then there was nothing. Now here I was back in the present, unsure of how much time had passed, but definitely feeling more pain than I ever had in my life. There was no part on my body that didn't ache bad enough to make me understand that death would've been a kinder thing.

I dared not move, I simply laid as still as I could and tried to take a mental inventory of what was left of me. Despite the fact that everything hurting on me indicated I was still alive, I knew I must not be far from death's door because the noises I was hearing could only mean I was in the hospital. The beeps and whooshes of the machines sounded like car alarms going off, but this over sensitivity was probably just one of my ailments. Trying to open my eyes proved all but unsuccessful because only the right one cracked a slit, and it was still hard to see around all the blood caked into my eyelashes.

My face felt as big and round as a watermelon, but a lot more deformed. It was hard to breath despite the tubes shoved up my nose, and I had to continuously remind myself not to panic or I might risk suffocating myself. As for the rest of my body there was no real way to take stock of my injuries because everything hurt. I knew there was an I.V. in my left arm, but my right arm was in a cast from my shoulder to my fingers. All in all, they'd definitely got their money's worth out of me.

"Mr. Vargas, are you awake?"

I heard a high-pitched voice call out. When I went to open my mouth, I felt immediate pain that caused me to moan, and the taste of blood was so potent that it took considerable effort not to gag.

"It's okay, don't talk. I'm just gonna check your vitals and then I'll get your doctor for you."

With my limited vision, I could make out a petite brunette wearing purple nurses' scrubs, and she was looking at the machines I was hooked up to. I was hoping she'd administer some good dope, but all I saw in her hands was a clipboard and a pen for note taking. Her movements were methodical, but not hurried which I took to mean that I wasn't going to die at the moment. Given the fact that I still had to walk, or be carried back into the same lion's den where this all started I wasn't sure how grateful to feel for my life.

I wasn't one to pity myself, but even I had to admit how slim my odds of survival were in that jail. Laying here in agony my mind actually cleared enough for me to see how well Zayvion had played his hand. Not only did he get out of prison, but he managed to put a target on my back without spending a dollar to do it. Having him stabbed on the inside had run me $10,000, and the mufucka was still alive! That was okay though because I was gonna figure a way out of this mess, and then I'd deal with him with my own two hands.

"What do we have, Abby?"

A slim built black man in a white lab coat asked, coming from somewhere out of my field of vision.

"Mr. Vargas is awake, Dr. Undoko, and his vitals are steady."

"Good, good. Mr. Vargas, I'm sure you can hear me, but talking will prove both difficult and painful given your fractured jaw. Right now, I just want you to listen and we can try to get to any important questions in a moment. You were admitted into Fairfax hospital about 6 hours ago, following a fight you had with several drunks in a holding cell at the county jail. I'm not sure how much you remember because your CAT scan revealed some brain swelling, but thankfully, no bleeding of the brain. You have three broken ribs, one of which punctured your left lung, but we were able to operate swiftly and keep it from collapsing. There's no internal bleeding, and the rest of the damage appears to be cosmetic. You have torn ligaments in your left knee, your right arm was broken in three places, and I believe you lost a couple of teeth. All in all, you're lucky to be alive, and I'm sure it hurts like hell, but you'll survive. Enough about your injuries, let's talk rehabilitation because…"

"Uh, Doctor, I think you're forgetting one or two injuries," Nurse Abby whispered.

"Ah-uh, Mr. Vargas, there was extreme swelling to your groin area, so we'll need to monitor your urine to make sure there's no blood or permanent damage. And, uh, as you know we had to undress you to examine your entire body for injuries, and, well, we found some slight tearing in the anal cavity."

For a split second my mind went blank because I knew this nigga wasn't saying what I thought he was saying. As bad as it hurt to speak I still forced one word from my mouth.

"No."

"Before you panic let me be clear in saying that I don't think you were sexually assaulted, as least not with another man's penis. But, there could have been some slight object penetration or it could just as easily have been repeated kicking directly to your anus. In my opinion, it was not rape though."

Some might have found his words comforting, but the fear of not knowing was at the back of my brain, making it thump that much harder. What the fuck had they done to me? It was obvious they'd laid the groundwork to cover their asses by saying I'd been involved in some drunken brawl, but I didn't expect anything less. There was enough hate in my heart to kill them all, but I was smart enough to know I couldn't win this battle from the inside. I had to find a way out.

"Ph-phone call," I mumbled.

I saw the nurse look at the doctor, who in turn looked towards the door. No doubt there was a cop standing guard outside in case I tried to escape, or more likely in case I woke up and the job needed finishing.

"I'll have to check with…"

"No. C-cops did this," I growled in pain.

Even through my swollen eye I could see the surprise on both of their faces, but they'd have to be complete idiots to think all this could happen in a holding tank without a cop knowing. The doctor had kind brown eyes, but they were eyes that had seen the struggle of police brutality. He only had a few patches of gray throughout his hair and beard, but he was old enough to know that cops would get on a nigga's ass.

"Why-why would the cops do this or allow it to happen?" Abby asked Dr. Undoko. To this question, he looked at me.

"Th-think I k-killed a cop," I replied slowly.

The light of understanding dawned quick and clear in the good doctor's eyes, and for the first time I thought I might have some type of ally.

"Abby is gonna stay with you and give you a thorough going over to make sure your bandages don't need changing, and then she's gonna open up your morphine drip to relieve some of that pain. I'll keep the officer busy, make his call for him," Dr. Undoko whispered to her before heading for the door.

I could tell she was uncertain at first, and I thought she might've been following the doctor out of the room, but she reappeared by my bedside with a damp washcloth. Gently, she began to wipe my face and the cool touch of the cloth brought some much-needed relief. It allowed me to see better too and I got a good look at my nurse. She was attractive in that book wormish type of way with hair that hung just past her shoulders, and some square framed glasses that magnified her big brown eyes. She was a little on the skinny side, but her figure was nice for a white girl.

"I can't believe they did this to you," she commented, shaking her head.

"C-could've been worse."

"I don't see how. I was here when they brought you in and there was so much blood I didn't think you could still be alive. Lucky for you, you're a big guy."

"Hurts," I replied, wincing as she wiped at the left side of my face.

I still couldn't see out of that eye and it felt like my face was big enough to claim an extra dependent on my tax returns.

"Let me open up your morphine now before I start touching you anywhere else," she said, moving and adjusting something I couldn't see above my bed.

The way I was feeling I was gonna need half a brick of dope to stop feeling like I'd been sandwiched in between two 18-wheelers.

"Call?" I asked, doing my best to try and spot a phone in the room.

She glanced briefly at the door before pulling her cellphone from her pocket.

"Who am I calling?"

"Girl. Kat. Tell her what happened," I said thankful that I wasn't the one who had to talk.

"What's the number?"

As slow and clearly as I could I recited her number and prayed she'd answer the phone. It had been a few days since I'd talked to her, but she knew I never disappeared for long, because her spot was the one place I felt safe. I hadn't told her about my court date or the whole situation surrounding it, so all this shit was gonna be a shock.

"H-hello? Is this Kay?" Abby asked. "You don't know me, but I'm a nurse at Fairfax Hospital and I got your number from Mr. Raymond Vargas. He... What? Hold on, I'll ask him. Is your name Rocko?" she asked me, putting her hand over the receiver.

"Yeah."

"Yes, it's Rocko. He was admitted after getting into a really bad fight while he was in police custody and... No, ma'am, I don't know why he is in police custody. I'm calling you because he's having trouble talking, but I think he wants you to come to the hospital. Room 418.

Okay, I'll tell him," she said, disconnecting the call and shaking her head.

"What?"

"She's on her way, she's very...animated."

I laughed at the assessment before I thought about the consequences, but the pain that shot through my body was enough to shut me right up. This young nurse didn't strike me as the type to be prejudiced or closed-minded, but when she said the word animated what I really heard was 'Ghetto.' The funny part was that she was absolutely right, because Kat was a project chick for real. She claimed to have left Jersey to escape the bullshit, but then she moved right to D.C. and somehow ended up fucking with a nigga like me.

There wasn't a hood across America that didn't have a chic like Kat in it. She wasn't that bad bitch who stayed up on all the latest gear, and was stingy with the pussy if you weren't spending that dope boy money. She was the one whose house you crept to at around 3 a.m. because you didn't want nobody to know you was fucking her. Certain chicks you could call ugly, but others you called a bugger in the back. What that meant is if you've ever picked your nose, I mean really get up in there, and you pull that slimy, nasty, crusted, bog mufucka out your nostril, that's a bugger in the back.

Kat was that type of ugly. You couldn't tell her that though, because she swore the gap in her mouth wasn't a mile wide, and the tight ass spandex dresses she wore were perfect for her 400lb frame. She had a heart of gold though, and she was loyal, which was why I kept her around. Plus, I could stash 100 bricks in her crib and all she wanted in return was some dick and a couple value meals from Wendy's, not necessarily in that order.

"Are you feeling the morphine?" Abby asked, putting her phone away and picking the washcloth back up.

I did feel a strange buzzing in my body and my head didn't feel like a set of blown tweeters, so the dope must've kicked in.

"Yeah, it's better."

"Good, well let's get you cleaned up a little and check your bandages."

She started by checking my I.V. and the various cuts and scrapes, but it wasn't until she lifted my gown that I understood the full meaning of a thorough exam. In order to get to my lung, they'd had to cut me open and so she pushed my gown up to make sure my bandage was still good. Of course, the problem from my point of view was that I was asshole naked underneath, and now this chic had her hands on me. I didn't wanna embarrass myself.

"It looks like the swelling has gone down some, just tell me if it hurts when I touch you," she instructed.

Before I could question what she meant, she was gently taking my dick in her hands, watching my face for any sign of discomfort. I could definitely feel where those mufuckas had danced on me, but the softness of her hands was distracting from the pain. The fact that she didn't have gloves on didn't escape my attention either.

"Hurts a little," I said.

"You'll probably be sore for a while, but we need to make sure everything is working properly. I need you to try and go to the bathroom for me so hold on really quick."

She disappeared into the bathroom only to return with a foot tub, and inside the tub was a piss jug and a bottle of hand soap.

A Hustler's Deceit 2

"Okay this might hurt, but we need a urine sample to check for blood."

She put the tub and soap to the side, grabbed the piss jug, and put my dick in it like you would a gas nozzle into a car. Despite the fact that I had to piss it still took a minute because I was reluctant to feel the pain she'd warned about. Finally, the floodgates opened and I was relieved to only feel slight discomfort instead of straight agony.

"It-it's okay. Not too bad," I said.

"Good. Now we just need to do one last thing," she took the jug to the bathroom and stored it, and I heard her running water into the foot tub.

"Okay, now just relax," she said, coming back to my bedside, adding the washcloth and soap to the water.

Once she was lathered up she gently began to clean me, starting with my dick.

"A-Abby," I said in warning, but she didn't stop or flinch when I started to get hard beneath her touch.

"I told you we have to make sure everything is working properly. Normally, I wouldn't go to this extreme, but you've had a long day so just relax," she replied smiling.

It was too late to argue, because suddenly the rag was gone and it was just her soapy hands moving slowly up and down my shaft. I opened my mouth to warn her again, but all I could do was moan until I was unconscious again.

Aryanna

58

Chapter 7
Zay

I'd owned many beautiful things and seen places around the world that were breathtaking, but none compared to watching my little angel sleep. It had taken hours to get her into this position, because she fought it with an iron will, but eventually her little body had enough. The pure joy on her face when I walked into her daycare center to pick her up was something I'd remember and carry with me always. Despite the minor breakthrough I'd had with Carmen she hadn't told me where we were going until we'd gotten there. And when I finally had our little girl in my arms, I watched all the anger in her fade, as tears of joy took its place.

I knew she was still hurt, but I knew how much our family meant to her too. For the rest of the day we'd been inseparable, first going shopping and actually sharing a meal together that didn't come from a vending machine, and then to Chuck E Cheese where we partied like it was Ariel's birthday. I knew niggas who took pride in buying out the bar, but I bought out Chuck E Cheese! A few times I caught Carmen looking sullen or staring off into space, but overall, I knew she was happy to have me home.

Despite my willingness to feed another bitch this dick I really loved my wife, and it was because of that love that her plea from earlier still haunted the corners of my mind. I didn't feel bad for what I'd done to Rocko, because when you played pussy you got fucked, but I did feel some type of way about how it affected Carmen. I'd always done my best to give her whatever she asked for, whether that be another kid or this nice house out here in the suburbs of Leesburg, Virginia. I did my best to treat her like a queen, but what she was asking for now bordered on impossible.

It didn't matter if I recanted or refused to testify, because they have the hard evidence that linked Rocko to the murder. Carmen was smart enough to know that, and since I knew my wife I knew she was asking me to get it done by any means necessary. Not only did I not have time to focus on Rocko, because I had real business to get to, but even if I did make it happen, what was to stop that nigga from gunning for me once he was out? Carmen thought she could control him too, but the difference between him and I was that she was fucking me, without the power of pussy I doubted she could quench his thirst or payback. To me, Rocko was yesterday's problem and my focus right now was on the little girl in front of me sound asleep in her bed, as well as her siblings that were on the way. I had to protect my kids and provide for them, which meant I had to get back to work a.s.a.p.

After kissing Ariel one last time I quietly backed out of her room and went in search of my wife so we could have a much-needed conversation. We actually needed to have more than one conversation, but I'd be a goddamn fool to mention another bitch being pregnant by me. That could wait until that baby was 18 years old.

"You got any gin in there?" I asked, finding her at the kitchen table with a glass of orange juice.

"Don't I wish."

"How you feeling?" I asked, sitting next to her.

"Physically, I'm fine. Emotionally, well you should already know how bad my morning sickness gets," she replied, taking a sip from her glass.

"Don't worry, I'm here now to hold your hair back."

"That's sweet, but that ain't what I need from you, Zavion. I need you to fix this situation."

"Look Ima be real with you, your brother ain't my main concern right now, it's about you and these kids. I know you ain't trying to hear that, but I don't owe you no lies," I said sincerely.

She took her time taking another drink from her glass before meeting my gaze.

"So, what's your play, Zay?"

"I've gotta re-establish order and show that I'm still an asset instead of a liability. I gotta make sure my credibility is still good with my connects, because if it ain't…"

"And how are you gonna do that?" she asked.

"For starters, I gotta clean house and show that I got shit under control before I'm summoned for a sit down."

"Sounds like you're up against a clock."

"I am, and that's why I've gotta go tonight," I said, bracing for the argument I knew would come.

"*Tonight?* Zayvion, it's one o'clock in the morning and you just got out of prison today! How can you even think about disappearing after all the time you've been away from me and your daughter?"

"Babe, it's not something I want to do, it's something I have to do. Word ain't hit the street yet that I'm out, but by the time it does reach the right people I need shit to look like business as usual. You know I want nothing more than to spend my time with you and Ariel, but the niggas I fuck with ain't playing and this is as serious as it gets. I know you understand that," I replied reasonably.

I could see the anger in her eyes, but she didn't say anything and took another drink of orange juice instead. She wasn't green to how this life worked, so she knew mufuckas would be looking at me sideways because of how quickly I came from under those indictments. Plus, there was no telling what dirt Rocko would try to throw. My only advantage was in the fact that I understood that talk was cheap and actions were the only things that mattered. I had to show I was still that nigga.

"How long will you be gone?" she asked softly.

"Hopefully a day or two at the most and then I'll be back until the big meeting is scheduled."

"You know Ariel is gonna be upset about you not being here when she wakes up. Just think about how hard she fought sleep because she wanted to spend time with you," she reminded me.

I couldn't argue against the truth in what she was saying, but I had to think about my daughter's future and not simply the moment.

"Tell her that I woke up early to buy her something special for being such a good girl while I was gone."

"You want me to lie to our daughter?"

"Come on, Carmen, don't be difficult right now," I said, trying to contain my frustration. It wasn't that I felt good about lying to my daughter nor was it an easy thing to do, but my complete focus at the moment had to be on survival. Why couldn't she understand that?

"Difficult? Nigga, you lucky I'm wasting my time with you at all!"

"Yeah, whatever. I got work to do," I said, getting up and heading in the direction of our bedroom. I knew she was hurting and frustrated, but I didn't need no guilt trip right now for trying to keep us alive.

Going to our walk-in closet I grabbed a pair of black jeans and a long sleeve black shirt, and threw them on the bed. We kept a small safe in the closet and after punching in the code to open it I took out $25,000 in cash, and my

9mm Glock. I put everything with my clothes, grabbing what I needed for a shower, and went in search of some soothing hot water. The only positive thing about Carmen being mad at me was that she hadn't tried to get any dick, because I still smelled like Burnette.

Most niggas thought the most relaxing thing to do when you get out was to fuck something, but nothing beat a hot shower to wash the feeling of grime off you. It didn't matter how many showers you took a day on the inside, you never truly felt clean until you could wash your ass in your own home. I took my time and let the scolding hot water pound my body while I organized my thoughts and planned the next 12 hours.

There was so much to do, and I was so consumed by my thoughts that I didn't hear Carmen until she opened the shower door and stepped inside. Without a word, she took the washcloth and soap from my hands and began to slowly bathe herself. By no means was I sex deprived while I'd been locked up, but none of them bitches could hold a candle to my wife naked. My eyes slowly took in her 5'3 frame, noticing that she'd somehow managed to add more curves to that 140lbs I knew so well. I knew from personal experience that the child she was carrying would only make her body more of a stallion after she delivered.

"Damn, I missed you," I said, closing the distance between us.

"Did you?" she replied nonchalantly.

"I can show you better than I can tell you."

She took my words as the invitation they were meant to be and grabbed ahold of my dick with one soapy hand. I'd expected her touch to be gentle, but she had a grip on me as she stroked me to complete hardness within seconds.

"Slow down, babe, or it's gonna be over before I get up in you," I warned.

"No, it won't," she said, smiling at me for the first time.

I'd expected to find her eyes full of lust, but what I saw was defiance. I didn't understand it until I went to pull her into my arms and she stepped back, letting my dick go in the process.

"B-Babe, what's wrong?" I asked.

"You want some pussy, huh? Well, I want a promise."

"What kind of promise, I already put a ring on it."

"I want you to promise that after you make sure we're safe you'll do something about my brother," she said, stepping towards me enough to grab my dick again.

"I-I-I..."

I couldn't think because instead of simply fondling me she was squatting down and she had me in her mouth. She had absolutely no gag reflex and she was eating me up inch-by-inch, pure determination blazing from her eyes as they stared up into mine. When I tried to move my hands to her head she slapped them away and continued her achingly slow torture of pulling all the way back before making my dick completely disappear again.

"Okay-okay, baby, I-I-will," I finally stammered, feeling my moment of completion coming faster than a freight train.

"You promise?" she asked, going right back to work as soon as the words left her mouth.

"Yes! Yes, I-I s-swear!"

"Okay good," she said, quickly standing up.

"Wait, wait a minute, babe, I wasn't done."

"Oh, I know, but that ain't what you really want anyway," she replied, turning around and slowly bending all the way over until she was grabbing her ankles.

Suddenly, my mouth was dry, and the sight of her pretty, trimmed pussy winking at me had me frozen in place. It wasn't until she took one hand and reached up to spread her pussy lips that I snapped out of my trance and moved on her. I stepped into my first stroke with so much force that her head banged into the shower wall, but my hands were already on her hips, which made falling impossible.

"Zay..."

"Shut up," I ordered, wasting no time delivering jack-hammer blows that I was putting my whole body into.

The sounds of our wet skin colliding gave the impression of a first fight if anyone had been close enough to listen, but I could still hear her pussy talking to me as it gushed and clinched at my dick greedily.

"Unh! Unh! Zay-Zayvion! Shit!" she screamed.

In her mind, she'd probably thought this would be a quickie, but she was gonna learn today. As soon as I felt her first orgasm rock her I pulled out, spun her around to me, lifted her up against the shower wall and I was right back inside her. All she could do was lock her legs around me and hold on while I lifted up into her with enough force to rattle her teeth. The look in her eyes was no longer defiance. It was love and submission, and that fed the animal in me.

"Say it!" I demanded.

"I'm-I'm yours!"

"Say it and mean it!"

"Oh god, Zay, Zay, I'm yours!" she cried.

I knew the encore to her climax was moments away, but still I stopped long enough to carry her out of the still running shower and put her on the marble sink. Unlocking her legs from around my back I put them around my neck, forcing her to lean back as I dove dick first inside her sweet haven. Three pounding strokes later she came so hard I couldn't control myself and I was lost in a moment of mental ecstasy. Neither of us moved, we stayed locked together trying to catch our breath.

"You-you tried to hit our baby in the head," she accused me, smiling genuinely for the first time.

"Nah, I just wanted you to feel me."

"Oh, I felt you, and I still do. Are we taking this to the bedroom or what?"

"You know I'd love to, but I need to handle business," I replied, reluctantly backing away and pulling my dick out of her. There was a flash of disappointment in her eyes, but she quickly tucked it away.

"Yeah, I know. When you come back I'm locking your ass in the house for a month though."

"Agreed," I said, stepping back into the shower.

"You say that now, but that's because you think you're gonna put the dick on me. The only reason you got away with that this time is because I underestimated how long you'd last, but I won't do that again. Pussy runs this household, sweetheart," she declared, once again taking the washcloth and soap from my hand, and proceeding to bathe me.

I returned the favor and 30 minutes later I was dressed and out the door with a promise that I would try and make it back sometime today for Ariel's sake. As soon as I was behind the wheel I pulled out my phone and hit up my Lieutenant Boogey to let him know I was on my way, and what needed to happen. He was the one nigga I knew was still on my team, because he'd been the one to make sure I still had dope when I was inside. Rocko and I had been partners, but I believed in compartmentalizing like the mafia did, meaning everybody had a job to do. Boogey was short for 'The Boogey Man,' because when I put him on a nigga's ass that's who you thought was coming.

The only way you got the trust and respect of a good shooter was if he knew you were a shooter too. He might move for money, but until he knew you would pull that trigger yourself all you were was a money source. Boogey knew I was 'bout mine, and we both knew where enough of each other's skeletons were to keep that closet door welded shut. The spot we were meeting at was in Manassas, Virginia, and it was the only place we talked the type of business we had to discuss, because it was swept daily for surveillance.

I pulled up in front of the building in Cornerstone Apartments and spotted his black 2005 Expedition. My eyes stayed alert and on the move as I made my way to the third floor and tapped on the door.

"Damn, it's good to see you, bruh," he said letting me into the brightly lit room.

The nigga tied to the chair didn't look happy to see me.

Aryanna

Chapter 8
Carmen

Dick can make you forgive some terrible shit. Actually, to be more accurate, *good* dick can make you forgive some terrible shit! There was no doubt that I loved Zay, but he'd put my only brother on death row. Yet here I was giddy as a schoolgirl at 6 o'clock in the damn morning, still thinking about what he'd done to me a few hours ago. Part of me wanted to be ashamed of myself for giving his ass some, but the other part of me still remembered every earth-shattering blow he delivered, and it put a smile on my face. Had me asking myself if the nigga could do no wrong as I sipped my morning coffee. At least he promised to get Rocko out of the fucked up situation he was in, and if he didn't keep his word to no one else, I knew he'd keep it to me. Or I'd cut that good dick off!

Okay, a bitch might not go to that extreme, but Zay was smart enough to know that if he wanted to keep his family he better act right. What I needed to figure out was what happened after Rocko got out because there was no way he wouldn't want some type of revenge. It'd be too much to hope for that he learned a lesson about fucking with Zayvion, because I knew better than anyone how hardheaded my brother was. I couldn't have the niggas going to war though. Given their line of business they had enough enemies without fighting each other. The only thing I could see myself doing was demanding peace with serious consequences for whoever didn't comply. I just couldn't let myself become a slave to my man's penis.

"Mommy, where's daddy?" Ariel asked, coming into the kitchen rubbing the sleep out of her little eyes.

"Hey, sleepyhead, come here," I said, sitting my coffee cup down and opening my arms so she could climb onto my lap. "Daddy got up really early so he could go buy something special for his grump bear."

"When is he coming back?" she asked, looking from me to the front door and back.

I hated the position Zay put me in, because he knew how much his daughter loved and missed him. I understood though. He had to handle business.

"He won't be gone long, but he said you've been such a good girl that you deserve something special. It's a surprise."

I could see the uncertainty in my baby's eyes and it hurt my heart, but I knew the best thing I could do was distract her.

"How about you help mommy make breakfast before we get you ready for daycare? You want blueberry pancakes?"

"Uh huh."

"Okay, let's do it," I said, getting up and carrying her to the counter.

She loved cooking with me and by the time it was all said and done this distraction would carry her through to daycare. One thing I knew for sure was that I was gonna call Zay and make sure his ass at least came home to put his daughter to bed. We spent the next hour making pancakes and eggs, then we ate, and I got her ready for daycare. She didn't ask about her daddy again until I was dropping her off and she wanted to know if he was picking her up. The only thing I could think to tell her, was that she'd have to wait and see. Before I left the parking lot I made sure to send Zay a text letting him know how my morning had gone, and telling him to get the fuck back home a.s.a.p.

Just as I was putting my car in gear it dawned on me that Rocko hadn't called me like I told him to yesterday. Processing at the jail didn't take that damn long so he should've been in general population with access to the phone. I knew for sure he put me on his books. The only good thing about the county jail versus prison is that they allowed visitation every day from 8 a.m. to 3 p.m. It took me 45 minutes to make a 20-minute drive, but that was the consequences of rush hour in a busy city. Lucky for me there were only like 10 people there when I arrived, so it only took 15 minutes to sign in and wait to be called. Being that my visit was spur of the moment, I only had $500 cash I could put on his books, but he'd be okay with that for a second.

"Visitor for Vargas?" a Sheriff's deputy called out from the sign in the window.

"I'm here for Raymond Vargas," I confirmed, walking back to the window.

"Ma'am, inmate Vargas can't receive visitors at this time," a short black female said from over the deputy's shoulder.

A look at her shoulder revealed her captain's bars, and that was a damn good thing because I wanted answers.

"Why can't my brother have visits?"

"Because he's unavailable right now, but I'm sure when he's able to call…"

"And when will that be, because he was brought in almost 24 hours ago, so I should've heard from him," I said, getting the sense that there was a lot not being said.

"Ms. Vargas, he'll call you…"

"First off, my name is Mrs. Miller, and I strongly suggest you curve whatever bullshit your trying to kick my way. I got a lawyer on speed dial that can make your day long, Ms. Lewis," I said, looking at her nametag.

She already had a strong looking face for a female, and the screwed look she was giving me right now had me wondering how big her dick was.

"Give me a minute and let me see if I can find out what's going on," she said, disappearing into the depths of the jail beyond my vision.

A couple of deep breaths helped me keep my composure while I waited. I just had to pray Rocko hadn't showed his ass and ended up in the hole already. I was just about to ask the young deputy sitting in front of me when I noticed the captain coming back toward us.

"I'm not sure what happened, but your brother was admitted to the hospital not long after he arrived so…"

"What the fuck do you mean you're not sure what happened? Bitch, you better find out!" I barked, wishing this thick Plexiglas wasn't separating us so I could handle her rough.

"All I know is he's at Fairfax hospital and…"

Whatever else she was saying was irrelevant, so I let her explain it to my back as I turned on my heel and hurried out. I had a million questions and thoughts fighting for dominance in my brain, but I couldn't focus on any of them. Trying to remain calm did no good because I just kept seeing images of Rocko hurt or stabbed, and I knew how real the possibility was because of what happened to Zay. My fears caused me to break into a run and when I got behind the wheel of my car I left a trail of smoke and rubber behind me. I didn't give a fuck if the cops tried to pull me over, because it would be a high-speed chase out this bitch. Horns blared and tires squealed as I weaved through traffic and blew through red lights, but finally after 15 minutes I was sliding to a stop in front of the emergency room entrance.

"I'm looking for Raymond Vargas, what room is he in?" I demanded, running up on the nurse's desk.

"One moment," the young blonde nurse said, pushing her glasses up on her nose before hitting keys on the computers keyboard in front of her.

"Uh...are you related to Mr. Vargas?" she asked.

"I'm his sister, what room is he in?"

"Well, ma'am, he's not really allowed any visitors, because of his police custody status..."

"Listen to me, you little blonde haired bitch, if you don't tell me where my brother is you're gonna be a patient your goddamn self!"

"R-Room 418," she uttered, her fear plain to see behind her glasses.

I ran for the elevator, willing myself to calm down now that I was here because it was gonna take some finesse to get in to see him. If I was lucky it'd be a cute, young cop guarding him, because I damn sure wasn't above flirting to get what I wanted right now. As I got off on the fourth floor I cussed myself out for not thinking to bring my pistol, because I only spotted one cop sitting in front of a door at the far end of the hall. A daytime jailbreak wasn't ideal, but I would've risked it for my brother. Of course, Zayvion would've killed me when it was all over.

"I need to see Raymond Vargas," I said stopping directly in front of the cop, startling him awake from the nap he was taking.

He tilted his head back, which gave me a good look at his tired brown eyes and full gray beard. Flirting might not get me far with this old white man, but hopefully some straight talk would.

"Before you say anything, Officer Turner, I know he's not supposed to receive visits, but I just found out my brother was even in the hospital. I promise I won't stay long. I really just wanna make sure he's okay," I pleaded.

"I can understand you wanting to check on your family, but we got rules and regulations that must be followed, ma'am."

"Look, man…"

"Hold on now, before you get bent out of shape, you gotta understand I don't make the rules and I'm sorry. Now if you'll excuse me I've gotta go to the bathroom, my bladder ain't what it used to be," he replied, giving me a wink.

I mouthed the words thank you and waited until he disappeared around the corner before I opened the door to 418. I'd mentally prepared myself for a lot of things, but what I saw were too many extremes to prepare for. My big brother was barely recognizable. His face was beat to shit, his left leg was elevated in a sling, and he had a cast so big on his right arm that it looked like the whole damn arm could come off! The pain of his injuries could only be described as excruciating, but it was obvious he was feeling good because there was a big bitch with her head in his lap gobbling dick like it contained oxygen.

"What the fuck?" I said, letting the door close behind me.

There was a loud smacking sound as ole girl popped the dick out her mouth, but the look she was giving me was territorial opposed to embarrassment.

"Who the fuck are you?" she asked.

"I'm his sister, who the fuck are you?"

Before she answered she looked up at Rocko, who nodded his head that I was telling the truth. Now most bitches kept a leash on their inner freak, but I could tell by the way she was eyeing the dick that she desperately wanted to get back to the music despite my presence.

"You mind giving us a minute," I said, becoming more irritated the longer she hovered.

"I should probably stay because it's hard for him to talk," she replied, finally pulling his gown down and taking the seat next to his bed.

"Yo, who are you?"

"I'm his girlfriend Kat," she said, proudly.

Immediately my eyes shot to the one I knew he could see out of, asking him if this bitch was dead ass serious.

"S-stay focused," he mumbled.

"Right. What the fuck happened, Rocko?" I asked, crossing the room to stand next to his bed.

"Five cops jumped on him and beat the shit out of him when he got to the jail."

"Cops? Why? What did you do?" I asked, confused.

"He ain't do shit, but being accused of killing a cop ain't exactly something that goes overlooked, especially out here."

I knew she was right, but I hadn't even considered the possibility of this happening. Then again, I hadn't considered my brother going to jail for no shit like this either.

"How bad are you hurt, bruh?"

"Aside from what you see he's got broken ribs, a punctured lung, and a few other things," Kat said.

All I could do was shake my head and fight back the tears of anger and sadness. It hurt me to my heart to see my brother like this, and it had me pissed at Zayvion all over again. Taking out my phone I snapped a couple pictures of Rocko and sent them to Zay with a text that told him what happened, and that he better fix this.

"What are you doing?" Rocko asked.

"Don't worry 'bout it, we're gonna get you out of this mess, but until then we gotta figure out how to keep you safe."

"We?" he asked, giving me a look I couldn't quite read.

"Yeah...I talked to Zay and he promised..."

"Fuck him!" Rocko growled.

"Yeah, fuck him, he's the reason my baby is in this situation to begin with," Kat stated.

"Listen, I don't know you or what claim you think you have on my brother, but this is a family situation."

"I'm Rocko's family too so..."

"Bitch, because you swallow cum or get fucked don't make you family, so shut the fuck up, sit the fuck back, and play your position. I'm telling you now it's difficult to suck dick when your jaw is wired the fuck shut," I warned.

"Chill," Rocko slurred.

The look in her eyes said she thought she could take me because I was smaller than her, but I knew how to put the beats on a big bitch too. Right now, though my main concern was my brother.

"Listen, Rocko, you ain't gotta trust Zay or like him, but you know you can always count on me because I'll never leave you for dead. Let me help you. Please."

"How?" he asked.

"For starters, I'm getting you the best lawyer money can buy, and we're gonna figure out a way to keep you safe. What happened to you might actually help when it comes to getting you a bond or house arrest, even though your arraignment has probably been pushed back."

"I don't even understand why he's locked up, he didn't do it," Kat said.

"If you don't have nothing constructive to say then keep your mouth shut, damn," I said, trying to prevent myself from whooping her ass.

"Listen, you don't know me, but your brother be at my house every night, so I would know if he left to do some dirt. Once he's in for the night it's just us and our son."

"Son? My brother don't got no kids," I said, knowing now that this bitch would say anything to give him an alibi.

I was looking at my brother shaking my head when I caught a look in his eyes that hadn't been there. It almost looked like guilt.

"Rocko?" I said, asking him the question without asking, even though I knew the truth.

"She's right, Carmen. We do have a son."

Chapter 9
Zay

"I-I swear, Zay! I swear to God I've told you everything! Please!" he begged, sobbing, his face a bloody mixture of tears, snot, and the sweat that comes from real fear.

Lamichael Clark was a lot of things, but he wasn't no bitch. Some might disagree, because he offered up information about me to the feds, but just like with Sammy the Bull, that didn't take away from his body count. Being in this situation he no doubt regretted his actions, but he still had to pay the piper.

"So, what you're telling me is that all of you who were willing to testify against me were bribed or threatened into doing so by Rocko?" I asked.

"Y-Yes! Nobody wanted to flip on you, but with you gone and him in the streets we did what we had to do in order to save our families. The nigga chopped up Kristen's daughter in front of her!"

I knew Rocko could be ruthless, but that was some cold-hearted shit. I almost wondered if I was being told the truth, but after being nailed to the wall and then having various nails shot into your body with a nail gun for 5 hours I doubted a lie could be uttered. I hadn't nailed him to the wall for biblical effect, but more so because he'd tried to hang me out to dry and I wanted to return the favor. The fun hadn't really started though until I pulled out the buck knife and started the incision from his side around and through his stomach. A couple times he almost passed out, but for some reason the Boogey Man happened to keep a spare needle full of adrenaline handy.

"What do you think, Boog?" I asked the man sitting on the chair in the corner of the living room.

"I think we got all we're gonna get and that I'm tired of smelling this nigga shit and piss. Even with the plastic down the smell might linger in the carpet."

"You're worried about the wrong thing, my nigga. As for you, Lamichael, I appreciate your honesty and I'm sorry it had to end like this."

"Come on, Zay, I…"

His words were a waste of time, because I was already pulling the knife the rest of the way across his stomach, dumping his intestines at his feet. Stepping back so as to avoid the splatter I watched closely as the light in his eyes dimmed until it finally went out. I'd never been this type of heartless dude, but in order to survive I had to send a message to the streets that said I was here to stay. Before I'd ever let me or my family be preyed upon, I'd get gallons of blood on my hands without apology.

"So now what?" Boogey asked, lighting a Black and Mild.

"Now, I gotta get to everybody else who ran their dick suckers while I was gone."

"I can understand and even respect you wanting some get back, but you know the heat is gonna be on if these particular bodies start dropping."

"I know, but I ain't really got no choice, bruh. You know how this game go," I replied.

"You're right I do, and if it was anybody else I'd have to let them put their own work in, but you gotta be that exception. Niggas can eat without you, but we can eat better with you, which means you need to resume your spot at the head of the table. I know you'll put the work in, just like you know that I can handle the rest of the situation."

"You sure?" I asked.

"Come on, my nigga, it's nothing. And I know shit is time sensitive so I can get on it a.s.a.p. while you handle everything else. Plus, you know you need to spend time with Carmen after all the shit that's happened these last couple of months."

I knew he was definitely right about that last part, but the last text I got from her made me think she was gonna need some space. I had no sympathy for Rocko, despite the fact that he'd been fucked up. Shit, when you did fucked up things you could bet that bitch karma was paying close attention and keeping score. At the same time, I didn't feel like the world's greatest husband because of the way all this was affecting Carmen. It was never my intent to hurt her, but my intentions and actions might not line up for a while.

"Aight, I know you can handle everything, and Ima drop $100,000 on you for the job. Ima start trying to put shit back together, but in the meantime Ima keep flooding the prison with this dope."

"I got about eight bricks in the safe. How many you want?"

"Ima just take one for now because I don't wanna be riding around with all that. After I go see these hoes and get some shit established I'll have someone make a major move down there, so I don't gotta take that hour and a half drive dirty all the time," I replied.

"Cool, let me get it so you can get on the move."

While he did that I stood gazing at the remains of Lamichael Clark like he was a work of art in a gallery somewhere. Boogey would definitely handle everyone left, but he wouldn't waste time asking them a single question before ending their existence. Their lives were already over and they didn't even know it yet.

"Here you go," he said, tossing me a backpack.

"And this is yours," I said, wiping my fingerprints off the knife and returning it to him. "I'll wire you the money as soon as I get done with this dope."

"Aight, Ima get started by getting rid of this nigga. Be safe out there."

"No doubt," I replied, letting myself out of the apartment and making my way downstairs.

It's been a long time since I got to see the sunlight glisten off my candy paint job, and I was looking forward to just cruising. Truth be told, I was also looking forward to seeing Alexis too because I knew it would be some good pussy without all the drama that came with my wife at the moment. After stashing the backpack in the secret compartment in the trunk I hopped behind the wheel and took my show on the road. I made a quick stop at Burger King for some breakfast, and sent both Iesha and Burnette text messages that they'd be seeing me soon. I wanted to surprise Alexis though. It was my good fortune that all these chicks lived in the Richmond area, but I still had no idea what the hell I was gonna do with all of them.

As I got on the highway I tried to work out in my mind what position everybody would play. The simplest to figure out was Iesha because she was having my baby, but that made it more complicated because of Carmen. Alexis and I had planned to just run away together, but in the daylight, those seemed like the nighttime fantasies of a child. I had to be on some grown man shit. The time for playing games was long gone. Knowing this didn't make the words I had to speak formulate in my mind, and as my big caddy ate up the miles to my destination I began doubting those words would appear.

I didn't wanna hurt Alexis because I really had developed feelings for her, the future was just so uncertain. It took me almost two hours to make the hour and a half drive, but when you had work in the car you moved with caution. Pulling up in front of Alexis's townhouse I wondered if any of her kids would be home. We hadn't really discussed how their introduction to me would go, and I was a little nervous. Nevertheless, I hopped out of my car, took a deep breath, and headed to her front door. After ringing the doorbell, I turned around to keep my eyes on the street, not on some paranoid shit, but taking in my surroundings.

Despite me beating the charges I knew there was still a chance that the law would be watching me, but I doubted they'd assembled their surveillance team that fast after my surprise release.

"What the fuck are you doing here?" I asked.

"I should ask you the same thing, Miller, or better yet I should call the cops," Captain Fuller replied.

"Call the cops for what? I'm a free man, pussy, but you better tell me what you're doing here or Ima catch an assault charge."

"Babe, who's at the door?" I heard Alexis call before her face came into view over his right shoulder.

"Oh, so this is your man, Alexis? You fucking the captain too?" I asked.

"What do you mean too? What the fuck is he talking about and why is he at your door?" Captain Fuller asked looking at the wide-eyed Alexis. She looked like a beautiful, blind deer stuck in the headlights.

"Uh…he…uh…I…don't…um…I don't know why he's here."

"You don't know why I'm here? Bitch, I'm here because I been fucking you for weeks and we'd planned to be together, but you didn't tell me it'd be a threesome. I'm cool with two bitches, but two dicks is too many," I said.

"Wait, you slept with him?" the captain asked.

"I…no, I didn't, babe, I swear."

"You didn't? So, it's a lucky guess that I know about the horseshoe shaped birthmark on your left inner thigh?" I asked, smiling as her eyes got even bigger.

"Baby, he…"

She never got to finish that sentence before her boyfriend/boss lifted her off her feet with a vicious backhand. That was my cue to leave so I made my way back to my ride, the sounds of Alexis screaming and crying out for help echoing in the mid-morning air. I probably should've felt bad, but she played herself, and my name isn't captain save-a-hoe. I can only admit to myself how dumb I felt for falling for all the bullshit she kicked at me while I was locked up. The pussy had been so good that I had illusions that the emotions attached to it were real. That was a rookie mistake, but not one that couldn't be fixed or forgotten. I had other stops to make and other business to handle. That may have been selfish of me, but that was just life.

Chapter 10
Rocko
One month later...

"How you feeling today, Mr. Vargas?"

"Don't you think we're on a first name basis by now, Abby," I replied with a slight smile.

"Of course, but I had to make it sound good for the old man sitting guard in the hallway. You must be some kind of dangerous if they've got a guy who's at least a hundred watching you!"

"I know right. P.T. is a good old boy though, and given his age I believe him when he refers to himself as the legend," I said, laughing softly.

"Is he the one taking you to court today?"

"Yeah, but they'll definitely send more than him given how high profile my case is."

"I still can't believe you'd do something like that. I mean, I know I've only known you a month, but you don't seem like the type to kill anybody," she said, moving around and checking my vitals against the chart in her hands.

"You're just saying that because you're sweet on me."

"Oh, shut up," she replied laughing and swatting me playfully on the leg with my chart.

It had been a long month in the hospital trying to heal, but it was damn sure better than being in jail. The food still sucked, but I got the company of the beautiful Abby five days a week, and every now and then she'd sneak me some fast food. A couple of times she even let me eat her and she was mmm mmm good.

Aside from the extra, she made sure I got the medical attention I needed, which went a long way towards me being about 80% healed. I still had the cast on my right arm, and my left knee was sporting a brace, but the pain had subsided in a major way. I hadn't just spent the last month healing though, I'd been plotting. Carmen stayed true to her word and got me a wolf for a lawyer, a young chick named Valerie Berkson from New York. The first time I'd seen her I thought she was a joke. I mean she was 5'2 with heels on, jet black hair, with an okay body hidden under a business suit that looked like it could've been her mom's.

In my mind, I been cussing Carmen out for bringing me a little kid like my life wasn't on the line, but then I'd had a conversation with her. Not only was she smart, and came with a helluva trial track record, but she knew she was constantly judged by her appearance and she used it to her advantage.

"What time is it?" I asked.

"It's quarter after nine, what time do you gotta be in court?"

"Eleven, but my lawyer will be here early because she's not letting me be escorted without her seeing how the cops handle me."

"Shit, I don't blame her with the way they did you last time you were unsupervised. I don't think you know how close you were to death."

But I did know, and that's why part of the plan I'd concocted in the last month included good ole Sergeant Jimmy. For his sake, he'd better pray I didn't get out in the near future because that would be his entire ass.

"What does your lawyer expect to happen?" Abby asked, pulling up a chair next to my bed.

"Well, this is just the preliminary, but we'll find out exactly how bad shit is and what evidence they have."

"Do you think you'll beat it?"

"Honestly, I've underestimated the mufucka who set it up at every turn, but I've been giving it some serious thought. If he put this much thought into it 5 years ago, before he even knew how I truly felt, then he probably didn't leave any loopholes. The gun has my print on it and it's definitely the murder weapon, plus they've got him saying I confessed, unless we can get them on a tech the best I can hope for is that my lawyer keeps me off death row."

"But that would still be life in prison, wouldn't it?" she asked softly.

"Yeah."

Doing day for day locked up until God called your number was never something you got used to, at least not in my opinion. I mean now how the hell do you just accept that? I'd been trying for the last month to wrap my head around it, but forever was a long time. Plus, it didn't help that every time Carmen came to see me she kept trying to convince me that Zayvion would keep his promise and get me out of this. She was so naïve to believe that bullshit he was kickin,' but if I had to choose between accepting that or life in prison, then I'd believe in Zay. I didn't see how he could fix it because the nigga most definitely wasn't falling on his sword, but if anyone knew how to get around the setup it was the one who orchestrated the whole damn thing.

"Hey, why the tears?" I asked, surprised by the emotion coming from Abby.

"I'm sorry. It's just that you don't deserve to spend the rest of your life in prison, you're a good man."

"I'm glad you think so, but sweetheart, you've only known me a month," I reminded her, passing her the tissue box off the table next to my bed.

"I'm not naïve, Rocko, I'm pretty sure you can handle yourself in the lifestyle you lead. I just don't think you're so messed up that you deserve a life sentence. What about your little boy, what happens to him if you're gone forever?"

The question she asked was the same one I'd been asking myself ever since the cold steel of the handcuffs hit my wrists and I was read my rights. Rocko Junior was only 4 years old so he didn't really understand what was going on, but just not seeing his dad every night was affecting him according to Kat. I'd kept his existence a secret because I never wanted him to be a part of this lifestyle, and I didn't want him or his mother to be a target. Carmen understood when I told her that, and vowed to keep my secret as well as provide for her nephew. But she wasn't his father, and no one could ever take my place or ease my son's pain. It was on me to find a way to take that pain away.

"Financially my son will be taken care of, but that's the only question I can answer right now. If I get a life sentence I'll use that time to continue being his dad from prison and hope that he learns from my mistakes. If I get the death penalty, well…"

"I don't even wanna talk or think like that, please," she said, shaking her head.

"Will you come visit me?" I asked with a smile.

"Maybe. I've never been inside a prison before, would I be safe?"

"Anywhere you go with me you'll be safe, don't worry."

"I believe you, but let's hope it doesn't come to that. For now, I know the doctor isn't signing off on your release, not until you're completely healed and able to defend yourself. So, I guess you're stuck with me," she said, giving me a sly smile.

That wasn't something either of us minded really. Aside from talking and getting to know each other, we'd gotten to know each other in more intimate ways. The hand job she'd given me had only been the beginning of our adventures, but she hadn't let me take her down yet. Her reasoning was that she was afraid to hurt me, but in truth I don't think she'd ever fucked a black dude before. I didn't have a lot of experience with white women, but everything I'd heard about their head game was the gospel. The first time we sixty-nined I'd thought death was around the corner, and from then on I'd had to imagine it was sweet, innocent Abby with my dick in her throat in order to cum when I was with Kat.

"So how am I doing recovering wise?" I asked.

"You look good. The cast will come off in a couple of weeks, and the x-rays that were taken yesterday show improved healing in your lung. How does your knee feel?"

"Not bad, physical therapy is a bitch though."

"Yeah, but you need it," she replied, sitting my chart down and getting up to inspect my knee in its brace.

"Bend it for me," she instructed.

"You just trying to peek under my gown."

"Oh please, I've already seen all you got," she replied laughing.

"Are you going to check me for selling today?"

"Do I need to?"

"I think…"

"Vargas, I got your attire for court here," Turner said, coming through the door with a fresh jail issued jumpsuit.

"Really, P.T., I can't just wear my hospital gown?"

"Afraid not, sir, but the good news is that I'm not gonna be the one to help you get dressed. Here you go," he said, handing the garment to Abby and retreating the way he'd come.

"Well, I guess that means you're my tailor now," I said smiling.

"Ugh, my job is never done. You better help me though."

"I'll do what I can," I replied, hitting the buttons to lower the bed to the floor to make standing easier.

Once I was on my feet I used my good arm to pull my gown over my head, which left me standing in front of her completely naked.

"Okay, you're turn," I said.

"Very funny," she replied, handing me the jumpsuit.

Instead of taking it from her hands I took her wrist instead and pulled her closer to me.

"I wasn't trying to be funny, Abby, you know I want you, and I know you want the same thing."

"Rocko, I…"

Whatever she was gonna say was silenced when my lips found her incredibly soft ones. Once she dropped the jumpsuit, I pulled her body firmly up against mine as I explored her mouth thoroughly. We hadn't spent a lot of time kissing in the past, and right now I was wondering why not because she was damn good at it. It was hard to pull her into the embrace I wanted because of my cast, but I still had enough mobility to work her pants and panties down over her hips.

"W-wait, Rocko, we can't."

"We can, baby, we can," I said, breathing heavily, my fingers already dancing with her clit and knocking down the doors guarding her delicious nectar. I barely got one finger inside her tight, throbbing, wetness before she was clinging to me with her nails in my back.

"I'll be gentle, baby, I promise," I said, turning her around until the bed was behind her.

I could see uncertainty swimming in her beautiful brown eyes, but more than that was an unbridled hunger. I didn't meet any resistance when I helped her lay down or when I slid one leg out of her pants and panties. I loved how neat she kept her pussy with just a narrow strip of hair, and she always smelled like sweet apples. When I pulled her to the edge of the bed and stepped in between her legs I saw her eyes widen at the sight of my dick.

"I'll go as slow as you need me to," I said, pushing just the head inside her to gauge her response.

Slow and steady I worked my way all the way inside her, but I didn't move after that.

"You okay?" I asked.

"Y-Yeah."

The suction was so strong when I pulled back out of her that it took my breath away and for a split second I lost control as I quickly dove back inside her. Her beautiful face was full of surprise and wonder, but no regret. She may not have been a virgin, but her pussy was tight enough to make me know that if I went too fast I'd cum instantly. With this in mind, I set a relaxed pace, but we were no more than 10 strokes in when I felt her whole body start shaking and she came all over me. She had both hands over her mouth to keep from screaming out, but now I was like a shark with blood in the water.

"Wrap your legs around me," I ordered, fucking her harder and loving the wet smacking sound her pussy was kicking at me with each blow delivered.

"Rock-o! Rock-Rock-ohhh!" She moaned in a strangled whisper.

I wanted to bend her up and knock her guts loose, but I couldn't do that with one arm. Still, I pounded her faster and harder, chasing my climax.

"Vargas, you ready...whoa! That's thirty days in the hole when you get to the jail," I heard P.T. say laughing, and then I heard the door close.

"Stop, stop, Rocko!" Abby said, pushing me back as she sat up.

"He's gone, Abby, why are we stopping?"

"Because if he says anything I'll lose my job! I can't believe we got caught."

"It's okay, he's not gonna say shit and even if he did I can take care of you."

"I don't need to be one of your kept women, Rocko, that's not who I am," she said, getting dressed hurriedly.

"Come on, Abby, you know that's not what I meant."

I thought she'd give me a chance to talk to her, but she left me right there with a hard dick as frustrated as I was. Shaking my head I picked up the jumpsuit and began struggling into it. I'd just got it on and zipped when P.T. walked in with my lawyer and two other cops. I watched Valerie wrinkle her nose and give me a knowing look, but my focus was on all the jewelry the cops were carrying.

"How you think you gonna put all that shit on me?" I asked, holding up my cast for all to see.

"Don't worry, I've already straightened that out and you'll only have to wear leg irons," Valerie said.

I sat down on the bed so I could be fitted with shackles, and then I shuffled into the hallway where I found a wheelchair and two more cops.

"So, you don't accidentally fall," Valerie said from behind me.

It would seem that she'd thought of everything, so I took a seat and allowed myself to be pushed down the hall to the elevator.

"I'll be following behind the police transport van in my car all the way to the courthouse," Valerie told me once we were outside in front of the hospital.

She stood right there while I was loaded into the back of the van before she climbed behind the wheel of her blue Lexus IS 300. As we pulled away I tried to get my mind right and focus on the upcoming court proceedings, but my mind kept spinning with thoughts of Abby. She was truly an amazing person, and I didn't feel that just because the pussy was fire. I had to make shit right when I got back.

My thoughts were suddenly interrupted by the sound of tires screeching, and then the windshield exploded right before the sounds of gunfire reached my ears. The driver and passenger were instant lunchmeat, but my concern wasn't for them. The bullets were flying from all angles. I was boxed in with nowhere to run.

Chapter 11
Carmen

Any woman whose had a kid will tell you that when they were pregnant there were two things that became more important than anything in the world: sleeping and eating. To fuck with a pregnant bitch's sleep or her food was to ask for death a thousand times over, and we would gladly oblige. Luckily for me, I had a new man who paid attention and he'd learned these valuable lessons the first time around with Ariel. The proof of this was that my sleep was disturbed, but only by the smells of the breakfast he was in the kitchen fixing me.

Lying there with my eyes closed I inhaled deeply and took in the smells of fried potatoes, steak, and eggs, almost tasting it already. Lord knows Zay got on my last mufuckin' nerve sometimes, but that man knew how to take care of me and put a smile on my face. Most of the time it was with that toe-popping pipe he laid, but other times, times like this was just his thoughtfulness. A month ago, I'd had my worries that he was gonna be on some one track mind shit and be focused only on business all the time. He'd surprised me though by finding his balance. In fact, he stayed home more with me and our daughter than he ever had before. I wish I could take all the credit for this change in him, but I knew the streets were bleeding because of his orders and he was simply being smart by creating distance. That didn't mean I wasn't gonna enjoy it though.

"That big ass smile on your face tells me you're not asleep, unless you're dreaming about me."

"Sure, baby, you look way better than Denzel," I replied, opening my eyes to find my husband standing next to our bed wearing an apron and holding a tray.

"I detect sarcasm, maybe you don't want this breakfast I whipped up for you."

"Boy, you know better than to play with my food, so lay it on me," I replied, rolling over onto my back and scooting up so I was propped up against the headboard.

Gently, he sat the tray on my lap and my mouth instantly watered at the sight of the fluffy scrambled eggs, the well-done steak, the fried potatoes with onions, and the toast that was lightly buttered with apple jelly on the side. Beside the plate on the tray was a glass of orange juice and a single rose.

"Wow, babe, you didn't have to do all this. I feel like you might be trying to make up for something you did, or something you're about to do," I said, eyeing him with half-hearted suspicion.

"Nah, babe, nothing like that. I just did it because it's Tuesday and I love you."

"Well, I'm glad you love me," I said, picking up my fork and preparing to battle. "And I'll take care of that in a minute." I pointed to the apron that said kiss the cook with an arrow pointing down towards his dick.

I could see he was definitely naked beneath it too, which was fine with me because following sleep and food, sex was a must on the to-do list of pregnant women.

"I'm assuming you already took Grumpy Bear to daycare," I said, around a mouthful of eggs.

"Yeah, she didn't wanna go, but I got a few things to handle and I know you were talking about getting your hair done."

"I wanna get micro-braids so I won't have to fuck with it for like a year, but I don't know if my cousin Alicia can fit me in. I'd much rather spend the day with you though," I said, giving him a wink.

"Make a decision," he said, pulling the apron off and standing there, dick swinging not a foot from my plate.

I looked at my food, then at his one-eyed monster, then back to my food.

"You know I love you, right?" I asked, putting a piece of the tender steak in my mouth.

"Damn shame," he replied, laughing as he went into the bathroom.

I heard the shower come on and I was tempted to hop up and get a quickie, but my food was too good to get cold. It was okay though because I knew where he lived and his black ass belonged to me. Him being out of the house gave me a chance to make plans for the getaway I wanted, even though we hadn't exactly discussed it. With everything that was going on in the streets we needed some down time where we didn't have to look over our shoulders.

I hated to leave with my brother still locked up, but there was nothing to be done until his trial actually started. I'd wanted to go to the preliminary hearing to show my support, but he'd requested that I spend time with my nephew RJ. Rocko Junior looked just like his daddy, and he was a little bad ass too, but I loved him. I hadn't told Zay about him because Rocko hadn't wanted me to, even though I knew Zayvion would never hurt a child. I actually thought knowing Rocko had a child might soften Zay's position against Rocko and make him move faster. Zay knew what it was like to be away from an innocent child who depended on you for love, and I doubted he'd wish that on his worst enemy. Still, I wouldn't go against my brother's wishes, but I would look out for my nephew.

Finishing up my food and orange juice I sat the tray on the bed next to me and got up with one thing on my mind. Pulling my big t-shirt over my head as I went, I headed for the sound of the still running water figuring I could get the trifecta I was looking for after all.

"Uh huh, thought your ass was slick, didn't you?" he asked, meeting me at the door to the bathroom.

I was surprised to see he'd already dried off and now had the towel wrapped around his waist.

"I don't know what you're talking about, but why did you leave the shower on?" I asked.

"Because I figured you'd try to inhale your food and then try to entice me with the pussy. Sorry, but you made your decision, sweetheart," he replied, dropping a quick kiss on my lips and moving past me, making sure to smack my ass in the process.

"You'll pay for that later," I called after him, stepping into the shower to get my day started.

A refreshing forty-five minutes later I was out, and dressed in Zay's Kobe Bryant jersey and some jean shorts, with purple and gold Air Force Ones to match. I knew there was no need to look for Zay because he'd be long gone, but I saw he'd taken my tray away and cleaned up the kitchen before he left. God, I loved that man!

After grabbing everything I needed and putting it in my purse I was out the door and on the road. Rocko had kept Kat and RJ stashed out in Stafford, Virginia, which was only 30 minutes away, but before I went that way I wanted to go drop some money off at the hospital. I wasn't sure how serious shit was with him and this nurse he was dealing with, but she made sure he was taken care of and I wanted to thank her. I had to do it while he while he was at court, because he might tell me I was doing too much. I didn't see it as doing too much. I was simply doing what I could to make him comfortable.

I knew how ugly shit looked for him, and I was trying not to pressure Zayvion, but I couldn't take too much more of this waiting game. My brother needed to be home. It was just that simple. It took me almost an hour to get to the hospital, but that was because I really wasn't in a hurry. It was so nice outside that I was giving serious thought to going and getting Ariel to take her to D.C, but I'd have to call Zay and get the equivalent of a presidential detail. I get that there was an element of danger because of what was going on, but having all those bodyguards was a hassle.

As I was heading through the E.R. to the elevator to go to Abby's floor, I caught sight of her sitting in a chair outside of an emergency room cubicle.

"Hey Abby," I called, waving to her and heading in her direction.

When our eyes met, hers held a dazed expression almost like she didn't recognize me, but then it was like turning on a light switch. All of a sudden, she was out of her seat and moving in my direction. I thought she was coming to greet me, but she damn near tackled me with her embrace.

"Oh God, oh God," she moaned, crying almost hysterically.

I had no idea what the fuck was going on, but fear that bordered on terror was dancing up my spine.

"What's wrong? Abby, tell me what the fuck is going on!" I demanded, grabbing her by her shoulders and shaking her head.

"T-they didn't call you?"

"Who didn't call me, and for what?"

"It's-It's Rocko. He was being transported to court and they were attacked by masked gunmen. H-he was shot four times."

Shaking my head was an instinctive motion, because not only did I want to deny what she'd just said, but I wanted the screaming in my head to stop so I could think clearly. It wasn't until this very moment that I noticed the dried blood on Abby's scrubs and that somehow made the words she'd spoken that much more real.

"Is-is he…did they k-kill my brother?" I asked softly, fearing the answer as much as needing it to come quick like ripping a Band-Aid off.

"No, they're preparing him for surgery. When they brought him in…oh god, I came unglued. We-we-this morning was the first time we…and then I saw him lying there like that."

The tears and pain in her eyes were real, even though she'd only known him for a little while. I was feeling so much that I didn't know what to feel, almost like I was confused. First the cops had tried to beat my brother to death, and now here he was once again laying on a hospital table fighting for his life. I was sad and scared, but even more than that I was pissed.

"Were any of the shooters caught?" I asked.

"N-no. None of the cops even got a shot off, and they were all killed. Only the lawyer survived to tell the story because she was in her own car behind the van, and she described it as a hit. She said the shooters came out of nowhere from all sides and opened up, and that Rocko was lucky to only catch four bullets."

I didn't think he was lucky in anyway, except that he'd managed to survive. From the description given there was no doubt in my mind that this was a professional job to eliminate my brother. Sadly, my first thought was Zayvion. He'd been with me this morning, but his goons were only a phone call away. It didn't make sense though, and it wasn't just me not wanting to believe that my husband would hurt me this way after all he'd put me through. He had no reason to kill Rocko. I mean the shit he'd already done pretty much guaranteed his death if Zay didn't lift a finger to help him. So, that left me asking who gained from my brother being dead?

"I need you to stay as close to Rocko as you can, and keep your eyes open in case someone comes back to finish the job," I said.

"The cops sent more officers down here."

"The police are the last mufuckas I'd trust with my brother's life. Come with me to the bathroom," I said, leading the way. Once we were inside with the door locked I reached inside my purse and pulled out my pistol.

"Take this, it's legally registered to me."

"I-I don't know how to use a gun," she stammered, taking a step away from me.

"It's really easy, just flip this switch right here, point, and shoot anything that threatens Rocko."

I passed her the gun and watched as she clumsily tucked it into her scrubs. I found a pen and a piece of paper in my purse, wrote my number on it, and passed it to her.

"Call me as soon as he's out of surgery," I said.

"Wait, you're leaving?"

"Somebody just tried to assassinate my brother and if I can't find out who did it or why then I can't stop it from happening again. Keep your eyes on him and I'll handle the rest," I replied, leaving her in the bathroom.

I knew I needed to get with Zay so he could help me find the answers I needed, but first I had to reach Kat.

I made it to my car and was preparing to call her when I realized that this wasn't a convo to have over the phone. Immediately, I got on the road, calling Zay along the way, and damn near throwing my phone out the window when I didn't get an answer. Now was not the time for this nigga to go off the goddamn radar! I kept trying to call him even as my foot got heavier on the gas, but it kept going to voicemail. A bitch that didn't know her man would've thought the nigga was ducking out of guilt, but I knew that Zay conducted business like a lot of old school dudes who didn't allow cellphones around when discussing sensitive topics.

I put him out of my mind for the moment and tried to conjure up what words to use to break the news of what happened to Kat. It honestly seemed surreal to me that even one more thing could happen after the nightmare we'd all been living. I just hoped Kat didn't break down. It took an hour to get to her apartment, but my knocks went unanswered for five straight minutes. I called her and sent texts, but I got no response.

I was just about to leave when I thought to try the door knob. Sure enough it was unlocked. Before I even crossed the threshold the smell of blood hit me so hard that it was an immediate gut check. The warning bells of fear where banging loudly in my mind and I was definitely having a fight or flight moment. I had no idea what I'd find inside the apartment, but I knew whatever it was wouldn't be good for anybody. The entrance to the apartment opened up into the living room on my right and a kitchen/dining room on my left, and since I didn't see anything that could be responsible for what I was smelling, I continued walking down the dark hallway.

When I got to the open bedroom doorway the smell of blood intensified, but the mystery was solved because Kat was laid in the middle of her bed, her lifeless eyes staring at the ceiling. She was completely naked, and as I got closer I saw that her throat had been sliced so viciously that her head would likely roll off when the body was moved. The huge butcher knife was planted in her chest, but my focus was drawn to the note she was clutching. Very carefully I removed it and read it, then I read it again. If I was reading this right, then this shit was bigger than Zayvion. The note said Rocko was to plead guilty and keep his mouth shut, or RJ was dead too.

Chapter 12
Zay

"That's $100,000 right there, count it," I said, passing him the brown paper bag.

"I ain't gotta count it, bruh. I know your money good just like you know I'm good at what I do."

I couldn't deny that Iesha's young nigga Shmurda was damn good at knocking niggas heads off in a permanent way, and he didn't mind doing it. Even though I had Boogey on the team it still helped to bring in an out of town shooter every now and then. The Boogey Man had been about the cleanup while Shmurda had been about the takeover.

In the time I'd been gone a few niggas had tried to encroach on my territory, and I couldn't allow that to happen. It had been a bloody ass month, but aside from taking care of Lamichael myself, I'd made sure to keep my hands clean, and my face almost invisible. I'd even managed to make a legit move and buy my way into a trucking company. Now my guns were moving from New York to New Orleans and a lot of places in between uninterrupted. Since I'd proved to my EME, the Mexican mafia, connection that I could handle my business, I was back to getting my shipments from Mexico.

The Mexican mafia didn't play. Them mufuckas were absolutely ruthless, but they loved money. I'd been nervous about sitting down with them and explaining what had happened, but there was no way I couldn't explain. Like my cousin had said my indictments were serious, and everybody knew that. When I'd run my plan down to my man Hector, who was basically the shot caller for the East Coast, he'd actually called me a worthy adversary. He liked that I'd seen shit coming years in advance and I'd had a plan that didn't compromise them in any way. Of course he hadn't liked the fact that Rocko was still alive, but I assured him the state of Virginia was gonna serve up the death penalty.

What I neglected to mention was my wife wanting me to get Rocko out. I still didn't know how I was gonna pull that off without getting everybody killed, or if I even wanted to. The nigga deserved no sympathy or mercy from me.

"You staying down here?" Iesha asked Shmurda.

"Nah, I gotta shoot back to Louisville really quick and check on my baby mama, she pregnant."

"Yeah, that shit seems to be going around," Iesha replied rubbing her stomach and smiling at me.

She was barely showing, and she was beyond excited. I was excited too, but I did wonder what would happen when I told her Carmen was pregnant. When I was on the inside she'd understood the fact that I had a wife, but shit was different now that I was out and spending quality time with her. We did couples shit like lay up in the house and watch movies, or go out to dinner and do a little shopping. She'd even quit working at the prison because she knew I didn't approve, but she still supplied Trish with the work so my niggas on the inside could eat. I was playing house in two places, and eventually that shit was gonna catch up to me.

"Wait 'til you really start showing. I'm telling you my baby mama, Shaleek, is big as fuck," Shmurda said.

"You better not let her hear you say that," I said laughing.

"That's right. Baby, you still gonna love me when I'm huge?" Iesha asked, sitting on my lap as I sat on the couch.

I didn't know when we started throwing this love word around loosely, but I did love the baby inside her.

"Of course, sweetheart," I replied pulling her towards me for a kiss.

"And that's my cue to get up out of here," Shmurda said, shaking his head.

"Like you ain't never seen two mufuckas kiss before," she said, standing back up to walk him to the door.

"Of course, I have, but you my cousin. The only time Ima watch a bitch kiss is if I'm 'bout to get down with the party."

"Bye fool," she said, laughing.

While she was doing that, I picked my phone up off the coffee table, surprised to find at least a dozen missed phone calls from Carmen. I'd put my phone on silent because I hadn't wanted any interruptions while me and Shmurda discussed our next move. For Carmen to call me back to back like this meant something had to be wrong. I quickly called her back, but her phone just rang until the voicemail picked up. After trying two more times without getting through to her I began to feel something like apprehension.

"Zayvion, did you hear me?"

"Huh? What did you say?" I asked Iesha, who'd somehow managed to walk right up on me without me noticing.

"I said I'm hungry, negro."

"Order whatever you want, babe," I said, distracted by my efforts to reach Carmen again.

I was an hour and a half away, but if she didn't answer soon I was gonna be on the move.

"I don't wanna order anything, I want you to take me out. You ain't took me nowhere in a week, you just come down here to do business, fuck me, and go back to your wife, and you're barely even fucking me anymore!"

Was she really trying to have this conversation right now? I know firsthand how emotionally unstable pregnant women could be, but now wasn't the time for this shit.

"Iesha, don't start," I warned.

"I'm just saying, Zay, you ain't gotta treat me like a side bitch all the time, do you?"

"You right, you're not a side bitch. You're the side bitch I got pregnant and decided to take care of. You knew what this was from the jump, you read the fine print, so don't act like shit is supposed to change all of a sudden!" I replied heatedly.

"I'm not asking you to marry me, I'm just asking you to love me."

Her words drew my attention away from my phone long enough for me to look into her eyes, and in them I saw complete vulnerability. My anger vanished and was replaced with a feeling alien to me because it was a rare occasion that I felt guilt. I hadn't lied to Iesha at all, but I continued to have sex with her. Carrying my baby was emotional enough, but then I fed those emotions by continuing our relationship instead of trying to create a space where we could co-parent, I wasn't making shit easy. But truthfully, I didn't know if I could stop sleeping with her any more than I could say with absolute certainty that I didn't have love for her.

Just as I was getting ready to open my mouth to speak I got a text from Carmen saying I needed to come home immediately because we had to talk, but not over the phone. I didn't know what was going on, but I could surmise that it didn't have anything to do with our children. Not wanting to talk on the phone meant it had something to do with the streets. Putting my phone in my pocket I stood up to face Iesha. Her green eyes shined with unshed tears that I knew she wouldn't let fall, because she didn't want pity. She wanted love.

"You know there's love between us and you knew that long before I got out. I'm not gonna make you promises I can't keep, but I'll try to do better because I don't need you to be stressed while you're carrying my baby. I just got an important text and I gotta make a move, but I promise I'll be back this weekend and I'm all yours."

"The entire weekend?"

"From Friday to Sunday," I replied, pulling her into my arms and kissing her softly.

I could feel her melt against me, and as tempted as I was to lay her down and communicate body to body, I knew I couldn't because I had to go. I kissed her one more time and then I headed for the door.

Once I was behind the wheel of my car I sent Burnette a text that I was coming through really quick. She'd been upset that I hadn't showed up that first night, but since then we'd made up on several occasions, and now she worked for me. Every time I dropped dope off at Iesha's I made sure to hit Burnette off too and she carried it in to my cousin Ham. She didn't expect much for this service, just some dick and a few dollars, which was a fair exchange as far as I was concerned. I wasn't dropping shit off today though. I was picking up my money. The good thing about fucking with Burnette was that she never wanted to lay claim to me, for the reason I'd told her about Iesha. Plus, I didn't want her to run into her around the city and say some inadvertent shit. Within 25 minutes I was pulling up to Burnette's townhouse and knocking on her door.

"You got here quick, you must've been at Iesha's," she said, opening the door and stepping aside so I could enter.

The smell of weed was heavy in the air, but even if it hadn't been I would've known she was faded by the dazed, bloodshot look in her eyes. The fact that she only had on a big white t-shirt let me know exactly what time it was because when she got high the freak in her really came out.

"You got company?" I asked, stopping right inside the door.

"No, I was just trying to relax and get comfortable in case you had some time to kill."

"I wish I did, but I gotta get back up north a.s.a.p., because there's some shit going on."

"Oh. Well hold on while I grab the money," she said, disappearing upstairs.

Since I knew Burnette was a good chic I let her have her own Greendot card and handle money transactions herself, but I didn't want anything traced to me so I insisted on cash. Good chic or not, my trust was in short supply. A few minutes later she reappeared carrying a Nike shoebox.

"$72,000," she said, handing it to me.

"Cool. I'll make another drop in a few days. Do you need anything?"

"No, I'm good. I did wanna talk to you about something though."

"What's that?" I asked, wary of the change in her tone and demeanor.

"Your cousin, he…uh…came at me."

"What you mean he came at you?"

"Like he tried to holla at me sexually," she replied.

"And you said?"

"I laughed it off. I mean he's cute, but he's your cousin," she said.

It was on the tip of my tongue to tell her to do what she felt, but the look in her eyes stopped me. Suddenly, I felt like I was being tested and to fail could have lasting effects on my business. With my free hand, I grabbed a fist full of her t-shirt and pulled her towards me hard, capturing her lips with my own and kissing her passionately. When I was finished, she was gasping for breath, but the look in her eyes was unmistakable.

"You're mine," I said forcefully, before I turned around and walked back out the door to my car.

As I slid behind the wheel of my Caddy I saw her standing in her doorway with the door open and her fingers on her lips that were turned up in a smile. I sent Carmen a text and told her I was on my way and then I got on the road.

As I left Richmond my mind shifted away from the women I left there and focused more clearly on Carmen. Whatever had happened was undoubtedly bad, but I didn't have a guess as to what it was. I knew I was gonna be pissed if it wasn't a serious situation, because I'd planned to be in Richmond all day long. I'd wanted to tie up any loose ends before I took my trip to Philly and sat down with my weapons people. I still had a few days before I was expected up there, so if I had to come back to Richmond then so be it. Luckily, I didn't run into any traffic on my way back home and I made the drive in just over an hour.

"Carmen!" I called, walking into the house.

"In the kitchen!"

Following the sound of her voice I found her at the kitchen table with a row of saltine crackers and a glass of orange juice in front of her.

"Is the baby okay?" I asked immediately.

"Yeah, I'm just sick to my stomach."

"What's wrong, babe? What's going on?"

"Zayvion, I need to ask you something and if you ever loved me you'll be real with me and tell me the truth," she said calmly. A little too calmly.

"What is it, babe?"

"Did you, or any of your people, make a move against my brother?"

"No," I replied honestly, not liking the look she was giving me. For a full 60 seconds, she didn't speak or move, she simply stared at me.

"Are you gonna tell me what happened?" I asked.

"My brother's preliminary hearing was today. On his way to the courthouse his van was ambushed and he was shot four times. He ain't dead though. So, before he regains consciousness and tells me himself I'm gonna ask you again, did you move against Rocko?"

"And I'll say it again because obviously, you didn't hear me. No, I didn't and neither did my people," I replied.

"Then I need your help," she said passing me a blood-stained note.

I read it once, and then two more times, but it still wasn't making complete sense.

"Where did you get this, and who is RJ?"

"I got it from the lifeless fingers of RJ's mom, and RJ stands for Rocko Junior."

"When the hell did your brother have a kid?" I asked, completely shocked by this news.

"Four years ago. He kept it a secret because he didn't want him growing up in this life and he didn't want him to be a target. Now he's been taken and they're gonna kill him if Rocko doesn't plead guilty."

"Who took him?" I asked.

"I don't know. That's why I need your help. When I went to tell Rocko's baby mama about him being shot, I found her dead clutching this note, her head almost cut completely off with the knife stuck in her chest."

I'd been trying to process all the info she was throwing at me, but it wasn't until she described how Rocko's girl had died that the missing piece slid into place. I could feel sweat trickling down my spine as fear settled around my heart squeezing it mercilessly.

"Where's Ariel?" I asked.

"Still at daycare, why?"

"I gotta go! I gotta go get her!" I said, growing more frantic by the minute.

"Zay, you know something, I can see it. Talk to me."

"I gotta go get Ariel!"

"Zayvion, what the fuck is going on?"

"It's our connect, they don't trust Rocko to keep his mouth shut. I gotta go, because if they don't trust me...we're next."

Chapter 13
Carmen

Watching my husband strap on a bulletproof vest to pick up our daughter from daycare was the most disturbing and dysfunctional shit I'd ever seen. I wanted to go with him, but he instructed me to get the Tech-9 out of the safe, wait here, and not to open the door for nobody. I'd been around the streets life my whole life and I didn't scare easily, but Zay had me scared. Even without knowing exactly who his connect was, I'd known they weren't no joke, but to butcher a bitch and take her son was beyond savage.

I couldn't even entertain the thought of something happening to my little girl. It had briefly flashed in my mind as Zayvion walked out the door and I immediately ran to the bathroom where I threw up violently. I didn't give a fuck how powerful these people were, if they fucked with my daughter there were gonna have to kill me too. Abby had been texting me non-stop, but there was little to update me on because he was still in surgery.

Part of me wanted to tell Abby what happened so she could break the news to Rocko, but in my heart I knew that would've been some coward shit. I just didn't know how I was gonna look him in the face and say the words. The fact that Kat was dead and RJ had been kidnapped would destroy him, but even more than that would be the knowledge that he was helpless to do anything because he was locked up. I was his only ally and I had no idea how to fix this shit.

I took a sip of my orange juice hoping it would sooth the rawness in my throat, but I was afraid to eat anymore crackers in case my stomach decided to dance again. The sound of my phone vibrating on the kitchen table in front of me startled me so bad that I was reaching for the Tech instead of the phone. Once I read the text message though I felt the weight of a thousand bricks lift off my shoulders because Zay had Ariel and they were coming home. I had no doubt that Zayvion would do everything in his power to keep me and our children safe, now I just had to figure out a way to get him to care about Rocko Junior.

Trying to lay a guilt trip on him would only succeed in getting me cussed out, maybe even getting the shit slapped out of me. The situation was obviously past the point of using sex or head to convince him, but I was convinced that now more than ever Zay had to get Rocko out of this mess.

I felt my stomach lurch, and I grabbed the gun and ran for the bathroom. This time I only had the dry heaves, but I spent fifteen minutes on my knees praying either way. Once I finally regained my strength and my composure I made my way back into the kitchen just as the front door opened and in ran my beautiful little girl.

"Mommy!" she yelled in excitement, running full speed in my direction.

Scooping her up off her feet I hugged her as tight as I could without hurting her and just inhaled the smell of bubble gum on her skin.

"I missed you so much, Grumpy Bear."

"I missed you too, mommy. I'm hungry."

"Okay, well sit right here while I make you something to eat," I said, sitting her down at the kitchen table.

I signaled for Zay to follow me so we could talk.

"Tell me what's going on, Zay," I said softly so Ariel wouldn't overhear.

"I don't know, I'm only guessing right now."

116

"Okay, well tell me what you think it is."

"The people that we're dealing with don't like snitches, and they damn sure don't let them live. They never liked the fact that Rocko was locked up instead of eliminated, even though he's looking at either life in prison or the death penalty. They obviously want it to happen sooner, or at least for there to be no trial so he can't give them up," he said.

"You gotta get him out, Zay, at least that'll give him a fighting chance."

"Get him out? Bitch, have you lost your mind? If I help him what do you think they're gonna do to me, or you and Ariel? You better start thinking with your head and not your heart, unless you wanna die with Rocko and his baby mama."

"First of all, don't call me out of my goddamn name! And secondly, what the fuck am I supposed to do, Zayvion, just let my brother die? What about his son, your nephew? That boy is innocent, just like your own little girl sitting in there at that table," I said.

"Are you willing to trade that little boy's life for your daughter's?"

That question made me sick to my stomach again, and I wanted to cuss Zay out, but I could tell by the look in his eyes that he believed this was the decision we'd have to live with if he got involved. This shit was a real life catch 22 because I was damned if I did and damned if I didn't. How would I live with myself if I just let this shit play out? The guilt I would carry would be unbearable...but I'd be alive to carry it.

I busied my hands by getting everything I needed to make Ariel a peanut butter and jelly sandwich, but my mind was still a playground of complete chaos. Every time I looked over at Zayvion his face held the same expression and I wanted to slap it off his face, but I didn't see how that was gonna help my cause. I needed to reason with him, even if I had to beg.

"Zay…we've gotta do something. I mean, you didn't always hate Rocko, babe, and you could've just as easily killed him, but you didn't. You don't want him dead."

"What do you want me to do, Carmen?"

"I don't know. Talk to these people at least." Honestly, I didn't know what I wanted him to do. I only knew that it needed to be something. I was almost in a panic inside trying to figure out how to get my brother out of this mess and save my nephew's life. Zay was always a man who thought on his feet. I knew he could come up with something. In fact, I was counting on it. "They've even done business with you since you've been home, and you basically did the same shit Rocko did," I reminded him.

"The difference between me and your brother is that I was smarter," he replied smugly."

"What does that mean? There is no difference what you did to each other," I said becoming more and more frustrated.

"Fine, I'll contact them right now and ask for a sit down."

"Really?" I asked surprised, barely able to believe my ears, pausing in the middle of spreading peanut butter.

"Yeah. At the very least I'll find out if my assumptions are right and what happens next."

Hearing him speak those words lifted a burden off of me that was so heavy, its removal felt tangible. Sitting the knife and bread on the plate I ran into my husband's arms

118

and rained kisses all over his face as tears welled up in my eyes.

"Thank you so much, babe," I said sincerely.

"You know I got you. I'll get on top of that right now."

Not wanting to hold him up for a second, I let him go and went back to fixing my baby a snack, feeling more relieved than I had in a while. I only had one more obstacle to face. After I finished up Ariel's sandwich, and tore the crust off like she asked, I gave it to her along with a small bag of Cheetos and a Juicy Juice.

"Sit right there until you finish," I said, picking up my cellphone and going to the bedroom where I knew I'd find Zay.

He was on his phone, but he paused long enough to point at the Tech-9 I'd left on the bathroom floor next to the toilet. I picked it up and handed it to him, motioning for him to give me the Glock .19 he always carried. I didn't wanna be out riding around with a sub-machine gun, especially when I wasn't the one getting ready to walk into the lion's den. Taking the pistol, I went to the living room and slid it into my purse, and then I sent a text to Abby telling her I was on my way back up there.

Her response came back immediately because Rocko had made it out of surgery and was now back in his hospital room under heavy guard. She was gonna make sure that I was on the approved list for immediate family visits, because the cops weren't letting no one in who wasn't on the list. I was glad they were taking the threat to my brother's life seriously for once. Now I just had to figure out what to do about Ariel. On the one hand I didn't wanna let her out of my sight, but at the same time I couldn't take her to the hospital with me. Zay definitely couldn't play Mr. Mom right now, and aside from him I didn't really trust anyone at this point.

"So? What's good?" I asked him as he walked into the living room.

"I'm going to meet up with them in a few hours."

"Are you going to be safe going into this?" I asked, unsure of whether or not I'd made the right decision by asking this of him.

"There's never a guarantee of safety in situations like this, but the meeting will be in a public place."

"That's good, but we have another problem."

"What's that?" he asked.

"Where's she gonna go?" I replied, pointing to our daughter who was obviously enjoying her sandwich.

"What do you mean? She's gonna be with you."

"Babe, I'm going to the hospital so I can tell my brother what happened. He's out of surgery."

"Did you call the police when you were at ole girl's crib?" he asked.

"Yeah, but I didn't tell them anything about the note or Rocko."

"Which means you're the only one who can notify him," he concluded, clearly frustrated.

"I should be the one to tell him, babe, I'm the only family he got."

I could see he wanted to argue, and he probably had valid reasons like me being in harm's way, but in the end, he knew I'd go to my brother.

"Just hold up a minute while I make a call," he said, heading back towards the bedroom.

"All done, mommy!" Ariel said, getting down from her seat and coming over to me.

"That's good, sweetheart, now sit on the couch and watch cartoons," I said, grabbing the remote off the coffee table and turning on 60 inches of animated entertainment that would keep her occupied. It was times like this that I wished for more family so I knew there'd always be someone here for her.

My hand went to my stomach and the little one I was carrying now, and for the first time since I'd read those 2 lines on my pregnancy test I questioned the wisdom of bringing another child into this life we lived. I'd never had any illusions about who Zay was, or who my brother was for that matter, but I never could've anticipated their rise in the game to the level where bitches were slaughtered and kids snatched up. In the beginning, their lifestyle had been about survival, but now we had more money than we could spend, unless we wanted the government on our ass.

"Baby," Zay called, motioning for me to join him in the hallway out of earshot of Ariel.

"Yea?"

"I know you're in a hurry to get gone so I'm having a few of my people meet you at the hospital. You probably won't see them, but they'll be there. As for Ariel, Boogey is on his way over here."

"Boogey? Are you sure that's a good idea, Zayvion?" I asked, skeptically.

"Yeah, because I know that no matter what happens he'll protect her. They won't be at the house though. Before I leave I'm gonna have him take her to one of my safe houses, and once they're settled in he'll call me and then I'll go to my meeting."

"If you're sure, baby, I'll go with your decision, but as soon as I'm done with my brother I'm coming straight home so he can bring her home."

"No," he replied, shaking his head empathetically.

"No? What the fuck you mean no?" I asked.

"I want him to wait until after my meeting because if shit goes wrong they're gonna look for you both here. So, I want Ariel to stay with Boog and I want you to stay at the hospital until you hear from me. Understand?"

"I get what you're saying, just try not to be gone long," I replied, feeling guilt for even asking him to put his life on the line like this. There was no other way though.

"It shouldn't take long, babe. You better get going though." He gave me a quick kiss.

"I'll text you," I told him, going back into the living room and kissing Ariel on the top of her head before picking up my purse.

"You be good, baby, and mommy will be back in a little while."

"Okay," she replied, absently, absorbed in her cartoons.

Once I was out the door I quickly hopped in my car, making sure to keep my eyes open for anything or anyone that appeared to be out of the ordinary. I could feel paranoia creeping up my spine, but that was okay because it would make sure I paid attention to shit I would've considered trivial 24 hours ago. The first side effect of paranoia that I noticed was that it took me fifteen extra minutes to make it to the hospital because I took a different route that involved me doubling back.

As bad as I wanted to walk in the hospital with my gun I knew I couldn't because there were cops in there. I could only hope Abby still had my gun inside somewhere. I didn't see Abby in the E.R. so I took the elevator to the fourth floor. When I got off I thought I'd walked into a police substation because there were at least six cops in the small hallway, making it feel like twenty.

"I'm here to see my brother," I said approaching the group slowly so they wouldn't feel threatened.

"I.D." the one cop said stepping in front of me.

I'd anticipated this, which is why my driver's license had been the only thing I took out of my purse and put it in my pocket. Well, that and the note that I had tucked into my bra. When I handed over my license he passed it over his shoulder to another cop who compared it to a list he had.

"Arms up," the cop in front of me ordered, pulling a metal detector from behind him.

I complied with his request and he ran the wand all over my body.

"She's on the list," the cop behind him said, passing my license back.

Once it was handed to me I was allowed to pass and I walked into his room to find Abby sitting next to his bed, holding his hand. I could tell by the look in her eyes that she hadn't stopped crying since I'd last seen her, nevertheless I was still glad to see her. I didn't know who in the world I could trust with my brother's life, but it was clear to me that Abby was willing to put herself on the line for him and I appreciated that.

"How's he doing?" I asked, taking the chair on the opposite side of his bed.

"He's strong and he's hanging in there. I've been sitting here talking to him, asking him to come back to me."

"You and him have gotten close, huh?" I asked.

Her response was to nod her head as more tears slid soundlessly down her puffy cheeks.

"Don't worry, he's been through worse than this. Rocko is a survivor," I said, hoping that if I spoke those words aloud the truth would manifest.

"I believe that. I'm gonna give you some time with him while I finish up my shift, but I'll be back. If he wakes up, please hit the button so they can call me."

"I will. Hey, Abby, where's that thing I gave you earlier?" I asked.

"It's not far away. I'll be damned if I let something else happen to him."

Chapter 14
Rocko

It had to be true that God had a sense of humor because here I was laid up in a hospital bed again fighting for my life. I could complain about this, but the alternative was that I wake up dead, and that wouldn't have been fun. I had no idea how many slugs I'd caught or how long I'd been unconscious this time, but at least I hadn't regained consciousness in a world of pain like last time. Whatever dope they'd flooded me with had me riding on a cloud with my eyes closed, and I was pinned to the bed. It didn't affect my hearing though and the sound of someone sniffling forced me to lift my heavy eyelids to see who was wasting tears on me.

"You big softy," I said, my voice cracking and weak.

"Only when it comes to you. You're my favorite big brother."

"I'm your only big brother." I gave her a lazy smile.

The worry and fear I saw in Carmen's eyes was a new thing for me to witness. I knew that she knew I could handle myself, but so much had gone wrong lately it was possible the reality of my short life expectancy was weighing on her.

"Ain't no need to cry. It seems like God ain't ready for me yet. Or maybe it's the devil who ain't ready," I said, offering a weak smile.

"Not funny, nigga. Your black ass almost died again. I can't lose you, Rocko," she said wiping her tears away and fighting the tears in her throat.

"So, is it better for me to spend the rest of my life in a cage?"

I'd asked this question expecting to hear some more of the disillusioned bullshit her husband was peddling her about helping me out of the trick bag he'd put me in, but instead she looked away. Dying in prison wasn't on my bucket list, and for that very reason I had chosen to give up Zay, but I was realizing fast that dead was dead no matter where it happened. I didn't wanna die, but in the end no one cheated death, especially not in this lifestyle. Even with me being as high as I was I still knew Carmen not responding wasn't a good sign. I had no idea what had happened since I'd been shot, but it was obvious that something had.

"What? No reassuring words about my freedom?" I asked.

She opened her mouth to speak, but no words came out, and that left me with a feeling of emptiness.

"Zay must've finally told you that he couldn't or wouldn't unring this bell, huh? I shouldn't be surprised given how much preparation and planning went into getting me into this situation," I said bitterly. Yeah, I know I got this ball rollin' by turning on my boy, but every time I think how he'd been plotting on me for years, that shit just fucked me up. I been in these streets a long time and have done a lot of shit, but to go down for some mess I didn't do had me seeing red.

"It's not that, Rocko, it's… something else has happened and I just don't know how to tell you."

"Open your mouth and use your words. I'm so doped up that I don't know how many bullet holes are in me, so whatever you got to say will probably roll off like water off a duck's back."

The shine from the tears in her eyes were bright, making her pain evident. I hated for her to be in pain. She was

126

my little sister and it was my job to protect her, but I'd failed miserably. I could point the finger at Zayvion all I wanted, but the truth was that I'd let my greed get the better of me and now I was paying the price.

"Just say it, Carmen," I said, wanting to avoid the dramatic build up and pauses.

"Kat...Kat's dead," she replied.

I don't know why I thought she was joking, but I sat there waiting on her to crack some type of smile or say I got you. Neither of those things happened though. The tears that she'd held at bay finally found a path to travel down her beautiful face, but I didn't understand them because she hadn't even liked Kat.

"Where's my son?" I asked, my mind suddenly clearing of the narcotic fog as fear came crashing down on me.

The look in her eyes was no longer sadness, it was horror.

"Carmen, where the fuck is my son?"

Out of her bra she pulled a stained piece of paper and handed it to me. It took a lot of effort on my part to even use my left arm, but I managed to take the paper from her and open it. I felt my blood chill as the impact of the words written hit me with more force than any bullet ever had, but I still read them again.

"Where...where did you get this?" I asked, fighting the rising panic within me.

"It was in Kat's hand when...when I found her body."

"Who has my son, Carmen?"

"Zay thinks it's your connect, which probably means that they were the ones who tried to kill you."

"Zay thinks? Why the fuck should I believe him when he's the one who put me in handcuffs?" I raged.

"Because he didn't know about RJ or Kat, and he wouldn't do no shit like that."

"Wouldn't he? This is the same mufucka who framed me for murder, Carmen! We don't know this nigga. I told your ass that once already, but I guess as long as he keeps fucking you good you'll eat up anything, including his lies."

"Ima choose to understand the fact that you're hurting right now and not go off on your ass. But just so we're clear, that nigga *we don't know* is at this moment going to a sit down with whoever has your son to find out what can be done to save him. My nigga put his own head on the chopping block, because he doesn't know how these people feel about him right now. But because I asked he went. So, bite your tongue before speaking bullshit."

"How much danger is he really in if he's pulling all the strings? You not seeing clearly yo," I said, shaking my head in frustration. Maybe if I wasn't the one facing a possible death or life sentence I could be have the luxury of being philosophical. Right now, I was irritated beyond belief at her naiveté, and hoped it wouldn't come back to bite us all in the ass.

"Oh, but you are? That's a joke considering that you still trying to blame Zay for everything that's happened, like your own treachery didn't put you in this position. Nobody told you to kill a cop."

"For the last time, I didn't kill no goddamn cop! I don't know why you keep thinking I'm lying to you, because that ain't never been for us. I don't know why you'd believe that no good nigga over me either. You think shit is so sweet and he loves you so much, well why don't you go see Iesha and ask her how much Zayvion really loves you," I said, heatedly.

128

"What's that supposed to mean?" she asked, crossing her arms over her chest almost like she was trying to protect herself from the truth.

"Come on, sis, when the fuck did you become so blind to that niggas bullshit? Do you really think she was bringing him all that work and he wasn't putting dick in her?"

"He paid that bitch every time…"

"Yeah, in orgasms. He been fucking her, and god knows who else, since he been in there," I told her straight up. I knew she wouldn't understand what he really was. I knew the truth would hurt and I hated to give it to her like this, but until she could see dude for what he really was capable of we'd all be at risk.

"Nah, you just saying all this shit to get me not to trust my man. If he'd been fucking her you would've been let that cat out the bag. Plus, how the fuck would you know what was going on in prison while you were trying to take over the streets?" I could tell by the unshed tears and the rise in her voice that there was a war going on inside her.

Before opening my mouth to keep shit all the way real with her about her precious Zayvion, I hadn't anticipated this question, but I should've. If I said I was fucking Iesha too she'd see right through that lie, the same as if I said Iesha told me about the affair. If I wanted my sister to believe me and stop trusting Zay then the only thing I could do was give her more truth.

"I know because I was having him watched on the inside. I'm the one who put the price on him and got him stabbed."

For a second her eyes just went blank and a very loud silence hung between us. What I'd said would make her hate me on some level, because not only had I tried to get her husband and the father of her kids hit with a life sentence, but I'd tried to kill him on top of that. At the same time, she had to wonder that if I was telling the truth about this what else was I being honest about.

"You're...you're lying, you wouldn't do that," she replied.

My response was to look directly at her, because I knew if anybody could see the truth in my eyes it would be her.

"Oh God, you did," she whispered, grabbing her stomach.

Suddenly, she bolted out the chair and ran for the bathroom. The door didn't even shut before I heard vomit hitting the water like an Olympic swimmer. I know I should've felt bad, but I was still fighting against the hysteria about who had my little man and what they were planning to do with him. I'd seen too many movies like this, and none of them had a happy ending. What I was feeling went beyond helpless, but I had to accept the fact that there was only one thing I could do. Not surprisingly, I didn't feel as numb as I had when I first woke up, so it hurt when I reached for the button to summon the nurse on duty, but I got it done.

I was angry at myself for not protecting Kat like I'd promised her. If I was real with myself I had to admit that it probably was the Mexicans behind this. I definitely knew too much, but they should've known I'd never betray them or I would've done it already instead of destroying the only family I had. I admit I got caught up in all the money, but Zay had been my brother for years. The decision I'd had to make was impossible, but he was probably telling himself the same thing. Were either of us really justified? The answer to that really didn't matter now. All that mattered was my son.

"You okay?" I asked Carmen as she came out of the bathroom.

"What the fuck do you think? You're my brother and I trusted you more than anybody, and now you're sitting here telling me that not only was my nigga cheating, but you tried to kill him. Yo, who does that?"

"I'm not even gonna try to kick no bullshit at you, because whatever my intentions or motivations were I'm still wrong. You can be mad at me about that, but I need you to take care of my son. Please," I said sincerely.

There was so much pain in her eyes, but lurking behind that was an anger I was all too familiar with.

"Is he still fucking her? Because I know they're still doing business."

"I'm the wrong person to ask that question, Carmen, but you're smart enough to know the answer. Why don't you ask Iesha, and once you see I'm not lying about that maybe you'll believe me when I tell you that I didn't kill the cop," I said.

"Thank God you're awake!" Abby exclaimed, coming through the door and rushing to my side.

I didn't get to speak a word before her lips were on me and her tongue was forcing my mouth open. Despite the fact that I knew my breath was tart I enjoyed and indulged in her kiss because I knew it came from a genuine place of concern. I needed someone to care about me.

"Good to see you too. I wasn't really ready to leave the hospital, so I figured another near-death experience would be in order," I said, once she allowed me to take a breath.

"Not funny, Rocko. You almost died, and that would've killed me to see that," Abby replied seriously.

"What was hit exactly?" I asked.

"You were shot twice in the left leg, once in your already broken right arm, and once in the chest which of course went through one of your lungs," Abby said, wiping tears from her red eyes.

"I must have nine lives," I said smiling.

"I'm glad you're okay, but I gotta go, Rocko," Carmen said, heading for the door.

"You know what I gotta do, regardless of who has him. I can't risk his life."

"I got him, don't worry," she said, before opening the door and disappearing, leaving Abby and I alone.

"What was that about?"

In answer to her question I passed her the blood-stained note Carmen had given me, watching her face as she read it.

"Someone is th-threatening your son? Why?"

"Because in the business I used to be in I'm considered a loose end, and I know too much. They want to make sure I don't speak a word."

"So they want you to plead guilty? You can't do that, you'll die in prison!"

"What choice do I have, Abby? I'm supposed to choose my life over my son's? What type of man does that?"

Whoever said the truth hurts must've had Abby's face in mind, because she literally crumbled before my eyes, climbing into my hospital bed with me and crying in a way that was unsettling. In my lifetime prison had always been a reality, and you never get to choose how long you stay for. Had I processed what pleading guilty meant? No.

All I knew right now was that my son was in harm's way and it was my responsibility to get him out. Nothing was more important.

"Abby, stop crying, I don't want you wasting your tears on me."

"But…"

"No, listen to me. I knew the life I was choosing and the consequences of that choice, but my son is innocent. I know you think I'm a good man, but you only know one side of me."

"I accept every side of you though, and you told me you didn't kill that police officer, so why should you plead guilty?"

"Because there's a lot of shit I've done that I'll never be held accountable for. And because my son should never have to pay for my mistakes. Now the sooner you accept this the sooner we can move on to the next step," I said, stroking her hair gently.

"What's the next step?"

"I want you to call my lawyer and get her down here a.s.a.p. Her number is on the table next to you."

Reluctantly, she moved out of my embrace and grabbed my lawyer's business card and pulled her phone out of her pocket. I listened as she left a message telling her that I was out of surgery and awake, and I was requesting her presence immediately.

"What happens when she gets here?" Abby asked, once she'd disconnected the call.

"I tell her to wave my preliminary hearing and do her best to keep me off death row. A life sentence still equals forever because there's no parole in this state."

Hearing this she fell silent and simply laid against me. As much as I hurt for what happened to Kat it still felt good to have Abby next to me. She'd be the last woman I ever got close to. Accepting life or death wasn't something anyone could do easily, but I knew the rules of the game and at this point it was definitely checkmate. Mentally I had to accept this, but emotionally I wasn't equipped to deal with anything that happened.

"I h-have a gun your sister gave me."

"A gun? Why? Where?" I asked confused.

"It's somewhere I can get to it, and I think I can get it to you so you can…"

"No, sweetheart. I can't ask you to put your life on the line for me, and it won't do any good anyway. I've gotta do it their way," I said sadly.

"I know I'm not a part of this life you're caught up in, but I'd be lying if I said I didn't feel anything for you, Rocko. I trust my instincts when it comes to how I feel, so that means I'm gonna be by your side until you tell me to leave."

I didn't really have any words for what she said, because it was so unexpected. Here I was trying to mentally grasp what forever felt like and this woman beside me was offering to take a look at it with me.

"How old are you, Abby?"

"I'm 24, why?"

"Because you have your whole life in front of you, you can't waste it on me…"

"It's not a waste, and it's my choice so deal with it. Now, do you feel up to eating something?" she asked, changing the subject.

"Actually, I'm feeling some pain right now."

She reached up and hit the button that administered my pain medication, and within minutes I was ten feet tall and bulletproof.

"Damn, that's some good shit," I said, feeling sleep running down on me faster than Usain Bolt.

"After what you've been through you deserve the best, so just enjoy. When you wake up we'll eat dinner together."

"You're still gonna be here?" I asked softly.

"My shift is over and there's nowhere I'd rather be. I'm here for you, Rocko. Always."

Aryanna

Chapter 15
Zay

"Well, this is a surprise, I wasn't expecting you back so soon."

"I had some business to handle, so I figured I'd come check on you and the baby," I replied, stepping inside Iesha's apartment and closing the door.

"Is everything okay?"

"Nah, not really, but I didn't come here to talk about that. I feel bad about what happened between us earlier, and I just wanted you to know that I'm here for you and our baby," I said, sitting on the couch.

She sat next to me and took my hand, her eyes searching mine like she was looking for a secret or a catch to what I was saying.

"Zayvion, I don't doubt you as a man or as a father. That's not the impression I was trying to give you this morning. I can look at you and tell that something big has happened, and whatever it is it's affecting you, so talk to me."

I didn't consider myself a transparent person, but she damn sure saw right through me. I'd only survived these streets and this game by using ruthless calculation. When you did you couldn't afford to care about other people. You couldn't waste time wondering how your actions affected them because it was every man for himself when it came to survival. All my life I'd understood that, and accepted it as the cost of doing business, because the weak animal always gets eaten in the jungle. But this time I'd brought wolves to my door. This time my actions directly affected the woman I loved. This time I'd gone too far.

"You're right some shit did happen, which is what brought me to this part of Virginia this late at night. I'm just not sure how to deal with it," I confessed.

"Baby, I can't help you if you don't tell me what it is," she replied, squeezing my hand reassuringly.

Taking a deep breath, I prepared to give words to my turmoil.

"You know how I got out, and you know about all the shit with me and Rocko. Well, now that he's on trial for capital murder, my connect is nervous that he's gonna try to save his life by giving up their whole operation."

"Which means they're gonna try and kill him first," she said matter-of-factly.

"They already made a move against him this morning. Shot him 4 times, but he ain't dead. They took it a step farther though because they butchered his baby mama and kidnapped his son. They'll give his son back if he pleads guilty and avoids going to trial where he could give them up."

"H-how do you know all this?" she asked nervously.

"Relax, I didn't have shit to do with the murder or subsequent kidnapping, I didn't even know he had a kid until today. I know because I just came from a meeting with my connect to confirm my suspicions."

I could feel the slight trembling in her hand and I could see the fear in her eyes, but she wasn't scared of me. She was quickly realizing that she was in a similar situation as Kat because she was having my baby, and that joined us for life.

"I'm not gonna let anything happen to you, Iesha, I promise."

"How can you promise that? I mean what happens if they stop trusting you?" she asked.

"No one knows about you, and I'm trying to put together some type of escape plan now. I'm gonna keep you and our child safe, sweetheart," I said, pulling her into my arms.

We stayed wrapped in each other's embrace, our thoughts separate yet undoubtedly the same. Before I'd gone to meet Hector, I'd known who was behind the death and kidnapping, and my mind had already been working to figure out how I could get away with my family intact. In the movies, a nigga in my position always had a way out, but this wasn't a John Singleton flick. I couldn't ride down on the Mexican Mafia and kill everybody, and I couldn't politely ask to walk away either. I was in the game 'til the clock ran out.

"Do you believe Rocko will get his son back?"

"I don't know for real, but I know if they don't give him back that's gonna make my life a lot harder."

"What do you mean?"

"Carmen is crazy, and even though she doesn't know who my connect is, she's not gonna care if they do something to her nephew. She's gonna want blood, and I won't be able to stop her."

"So, what are you gonna do?" she asked, looking up at me.

That was the $10 million-dollar question. Hector had tried to lull me into a fake sense of security by telling me how important I was to their organization, and how we needed to keep business going smoothly. What he'd really been saying was that this was a warning to me because my black ass was expendable too. I'd never been dumb enough to think I was bulletproof, but having the mafia behind me made me move with the invincibility of the president. Having them as enemies made me more than a little nervous to say the least.

"How much money do you have saved?" I asked.

"Probably 'bout a quarter million, why?"

"Because I want you to save enough to disappear when I tell you to. Ima do my best to keep you a secret, but if shit hits the fan you take our baby and run."

"But…"

"No buts, Iesha, I want you to promise me," I said, looking at her seriously.

"I don't wanna go without you, dammit!"

The tears in her eyes surprised me, but I could tell her sadness was heartfelt. I didn't want her to be sad, scared, or anything other than relaxed because it wasn't good for her pregnancy. I was starting to regret my decision to tell her what was going on, but if she didn't know then she couldn't decide if she wanted to stick around.

"Don't cry," I said, kissing her gently and holding her tighter.

"I…I can't help it, Zay, I love you. Yes, I know you're married to Carmen and you have a family with her, but I don't know how not to love you. I'm pregnant with your child, because I love you. How can you ask me to leave you behind to die?"

"Because you gotta survive and give our child the best life possible, sweetheart. I can't stand the thought of what happened to Rocko's girl happening to you. I can't. Promise me you'll do what I'm asking you to do," I said, taking her face in my hands and forcing her to look me in the eye. I was trying to be cool and keep my head straight about all of this, but the truth is I was fucked up knowing that my ladies and children could become a target at any moment and I wasn't sure I could do anything about it.

Her tears came harder than a thunderstorm, making my heart heavy, but my resolve was strong. I had to know she wouldn't try no hero shit like taking on EME, because that was a whole different type of evil.

"I p-promise," she said, fighting the sob in her throat.

When I kissed her this time it was with passion and the desire to block everything from our minds except this moment. She tasted like the sweetest chocolate, and I couldn't get enough.

"How long can you stay?" she asked, backing away slightly, with a look of both longing and worry contorting her face.

"I'm not leaving you tonight," I replied, standing up and pulling her to her feet, and then scooping her up into my arms so I could carry her into the bedroom.

In the back of my mind I knew Carmen was expecting me home, despite the fact that it was almost midnight, but she had Ariel back at the house to keep her company. Iesha needed me, and I was gonna give her what she needed. Gently, I laid her on her queen-sized bed and began undressing her, starting with her jean shorts and panties. Before I moved to her upper body I pulled her to the edge of the bed and kneeled in front of her, taking my time so she could see what I was doing.

As I wrapped her legs around my head I could feel her heart beating hard, making her whole body tremble with anticipation, and I didn't disappoint. Using my tongue, I parted her pussy lips with a thorough lick, enjoying every drop of the delicious juices that found the back of my throat. I licked her slowly one more time before allowing my tongue to dance with her clit, which caused her to grab her sheets and hold on.

"Zay, baby please!" she moaned in passion, as I continued my introduction to her slippery goodness.

Putting both of my hands under her ass I pulled her towards me, submerging my face in the object of my feast, and I didn't stop until her cum quenched my thirst. Only then did I work my way upward, covering her body in wet kisses while pulling her tank top off. With her completely naked I stood over her and roamed every inch of her body with patient eyes, etching every curve and blemish into memory.

"I need you," I confessed, pulling my shirt over my head, and stepping out of my jeans and boxers while kicking my shoes off.

"You've got me, baby," she whispered, spreading her arms wide.

After scooting her back on the bed I climbed on top of her, at first just taking a moment to drink in her beauty in the moonlight. Our kisses held a sense of urgency, but I forced myself to move slow, putting only the head of my dick inside her before pulling back out.

"Baby, d-don't tease me," she said, locking her legs behind my back and pulling me all the way inside her.

Me wanting to set a slow pace had been more for me than her, because pregnant pussy could turn any pipe layer into a minuteman. From the first stroke, her pussy gushed an ocean at me while squeezing my dick tighter than a long lost love, threatening to make me cum within seconds.

"I-Iesha," I said, hoping she would hear the warning in my voice.

If she did she chose to ignore it by lifting her hips as I thrust downward, turning slow and steady into a pounding force.

"G spot…g-g-spot!" she cried out, digging her nails into my back, which brought out the animal in me.

When she moved her legs from around my back to around my neck I heard the bells of my climax in the distance, but I didn't slow down or stop. Grabbing ahold of her legs I spread them both wide, while putting all I had into the earth moving strokes that had her chanting my name like an Indian praying for rain. Her body bucked violently beneath mine right before she came with the force of a hurricane. I had no choice but to cum with her, but the night was far from over.

Scooping her into one arm I rolled onto my back without coming out of her, and she didn't miss a beat because she was riding this dick without hesitation. I let her cum twice before I flipped her on her hands and knees and let her pray while I blessed her with the shaft of black Jesus.

"I w-want you every…everywhere," she panted, spreading her ass cheeks wide.

Pulling out of the tsunami that was her pussy was a hard thing to do, but I did it and slowly worked my way inside her tight little asshole. Once I was balls deep I grabbed her by her hips and fucked her slow until I felt her open up completely to me, and then the party started. I rode her hard and without mercy just how she liked it until we finally collapsed beside each other, fighting for the limited oxygen in the room.

I thought after that round she'd let me sleep, but on this night, I learned why pussy ran the world, and on more than one occasion I thanked God for that. Before I knew it, it was 6 a.m. and the sun had definitely beat me home.

"You're trying to kill me, ain't you?" I asked, pulling her close to me.

"I just wanted to make the most of our night together. Plus, the dick is good," she replied laughing.

"You took advantage of me though, because you know I can't last long with how wet you be getting, with your pregnant ass."

"Nigga please, you only came fast the first time, anything after that you was just trying to kill a bitch."

"Baby, you know I'd never do anything to you like that," I said, faking surprise at her accusation.

"Yeah whatever, I know better. I guarantee my asshole is bleeding."

"You can't blame that on me, you the one who said you wanted me everywhere," I replied smiling.

"True."

"Besides, you know you loved it," I said, stroking her nipple gently through the sheet we were wrapped in.

"I did love it, but only because I love you."

When she spoke those words, I could feel her heart start to beat faster against my body, and I liked that feeling. Maybe it was possible to love two women at the same time.

"I love you too," I said, running my fingers up and down her arm lightly.

My words were true, even though I had no idea how everything would play out in the love triangle that was me, her, and Carmen. For better or worse Iesha was a part of my life, and there was no changing that. I wasn't naïve enough to believe that Carmen would accept me fucking with her, because shit like that only happened on white people TV shows. Still, I knew I was too far gone to choose, especially with two babies on the way. I hadn't played the hand I was dealt, I'd tried to rig the game. When you do that no one wins.

Chapter 16
Carmen
Six months later…

"How is he?" I asked, looking at the monitor.

"Your baby boy is healthy, and from the looks of things, just about ready to enter the world," Dr. Silver replied.

The sound of my little man's heart beating was like music to my ears, and I couldn't wait to finally meet him in a few weeks. Plus, the little nigga was hell on my bladder, so I wanted him up out the oven a.s.a.p.

"You doing the delivery, right Doc?" Zay asked.

I swear the nigga asked the same question every time we came to the doctor, so worried that another man was gonna get a look at my pussy. At first, I'd thought he was joking when he said Doctor Dara Silver was gonna be my new doctor, and then when I saw her I thought for sure the nigga was fucking her. 5'6, platinum blonde, blue/green eyes, with a perfect smile, and a big booty to match, she was definitely his type.

She had that porn star face that niggas loved to get their money shot on, but I'd be damned if that nigga was gonna have his hoe in my face. It took me actually sitting down with her and having a conversation before I felt comfortable that he wasn't fucking her, and only then did I care about her credentials. She was a good doctor and I felt confident about her bringing my baby boy into the world, even though his father was getting on my damn nerves.

"Yes, Mr. Miller, I'll be there as soon as the hospital notifies me that your wife is in labor. No matter the time or the weather," she replied.

"Dara, don't pay that fool no damn mind, he's worried about nothing while I'm worried about getting this baby out of me and staying in one piece," I said, grabbing a paper towel to wipe the gel off my stomach from my ultrasound, and pulling my big t-shirt back over my stomach.

"Baby, you'll deliver in one piece, but that mufuckin' music box between your legs is gonna stretch in a major way!" Zay said, laughing like an out of shape coochie was funny.

I knew he probably thought the hateful look I was giving him was because of his comment, but it was really because I was thinking about all the bitches he was probably fucking with pretty pussies. I was beyond the point of believing the nigga was faithful, because after I'd moved past the initial anger of what Rocko told me he'd done to Zay I thought back to that day in the hospital when Iesha had been there. I had my suspicions then, but I'd let this smooth-talking nigga here sell me a bridge in Brooklyn. I knew better now, and as soon as I dropped this baby I was gonna be on shorty's ass like a Las Vegas bookie about to collect.

"You ain't funny, nigga, so shut up and let's go. I'll see you in a few weeks, Doc." I said, climbing down off the exam table.

"Okay, and remember to walk as much as possible, and have plenty of sex," she encouraged with a wink.

"That's what I'm talking about, and babe, these are doctor's orders," Zay said.

"That's fine, Zayvion, but we're gonna practice with you wearing a condom, because after I have this little boy your ass is gonna wrap it up for a long while," I assured him.

146

"Aww, but babe…"

"Conversation over. Have a nice day, Dr. Silver," I said, opening the door to the exam room.

I could hear the doctor laughing behind me, and Zayvion sucking his teeth in frustration. He'd get over it though, because the truth was I didn't know where his dick was going when it walked out the front door. If he brought me anything back I'd kill him on the spot. Shit, the only time he got head was in the shower after I washed him thoroughly. Sometimes I felt stupid because I should've just left, but the reality was I wasn't giving up my man so some other bitch could have him.

I knew women who could understand that logic. Sometimes, when he was gone for a few days I almost worked up the courage to confront him when he came back, but then I remembered I was an uneducated black woman with two kids who'd never been more than a dope boy's girl. If I left Zayvion what would happen next? I mean, I knew he'd take care of the kids, but who was I if I wasn't Mrs. Zayvion Miller? An even better question was if I left would I look like fair game to Zay's enemies, or his friends?

He'd always done his best to protect his family, and he'd definitely avenge us if anything happened, but dead was dead and it wasn't no coming back. So, I chose the lesser of the two evils and stayed with the man I'd loved all my life, the man who was a good father and provider, and I hoped one day he'd wake the fuck up and see what he had before he lost it, or lost his life. On some real shit, it had crossed my mind more than once to go get some dick from one of the many niggas who hit on me, but I tried to respect myself and my relationship more than that.

Even being pregnant didn't stop a mufucka from trying to slide up in this good shit, but I wouldn't do that while I was carrying another man's child. I was mad, not trifling. After I popped little man out though shit was gonna change. I was gonna see to that.

"You wanna go get something to eat, babe?" Zay asked, opening the car door for me so I could slide my big ass into his even bigger Cadillac.

"If we do it's gonna have to be at the drive thru because I got somewhere to be," I replied.

"What you mean you got somewhere to be? Where you think your pregnant ass is going other than home?"

"I'm going to see my brother," I said, pulling my door closed before he could respond.

I could tell just by the speed in which he was moving to the driver's side that we were getting ready to argue, but he should've known he couldn't win.

"Carmen, I told you before that I didn't want you going inside that prison while you were pregnant," he said as soon as he got behind the wheel.

"I got pregnant inside that same prison, and you didn't seem to have a problem with that!"

"That ain't got shit to do with…"

"Look, man, I ain't seen my brother since he got there 3 months ago, and that's because you always make me feel like I'm a bad mom for going inside a prison pregnant. Rocko ain't gonna let shit happen to me, just like you wouldn't, and before you say anything, he got out of the hole for that fight he got into, so our visit will be contact. Say what you want, but I'm going," I stated plainly.

"Then I'm going with you."

"Oh yeah? And what about RJ and Ariel?" I asked.

"I can get someone to watch them and you know that. I'm going with you."

"No, you're not. Do you really think Rocko put you on his visitation list? He's doing a fucking life sentence because of you!" I reminded him loudly.

My brother was a sore subject between us to say the least. Once he'd pled guilty I'd gotten my nephew, but my brother's life was over, and when I thought about that it made me feel some type of way towards Zay. In the beginning of all this I had rationalized Zay's actions because of what Rocko had done, but ever since that convo I'd had with Rocko I'd been questioning who actually dropped the hammer on the cop. I had a vague memory of the night the cop was killed, and Zay said he was going out to handle business without Rocko, but he could've been lying because of what had been planned.

At the very least I knew Zay was involved, and he'd bought a new phone the next day. I understood why Rocko had pled guilty, but part of me would always blame my husband.

"Carmen, I don't wanna argue with you, so if you feel like this is something you gotta do then go ahead. I'll drive you home so you can get your car," he said, starting the engine and pulling out of the doctor's office parking lot.

I knew it was probably guilt that wouldn't allow him to argue further, not because of what he'd done to Rocko, but because of how it had hurt me. At the time he'd thought he was sparing me pain and protecting himself against what he'd anticipated, but he should've known it would blow up in his face. He never felt guilt about anything, because that's just how he was, but I knew he felt it now because he'd taken RJ without hesitation, and even had mufuckas looking out for Rocko on the inside. Of course, that came with somewhat of a price because Rocko had to keep his mouth shut about what Zayvion had done. It was worth it though.

We rode on in silence, making a quick stop at McDonald's to get me some fries and some chicken nuggets before heading home.

"How long are you gonna be there?" he asked, once we'd pulled up next to my car.

"Only a couple hours, babe, and then I'll be back for you to take me and the kids to dinner, and no Chuck E Cheese either, nigga," I replied, giving him a quick kiss before climbing out of the car.

I could feel his eyes on me as I got behind the wheel of my car, but I didn't look back as I cranked the engine and pulled off. I was determined not to feel guilty for wanting to spend time with my only brother because he needed me, and I'd be there for him just like he always was for me.

It took me two hours to make the drive to the prison, which still gave us three hours to visit if I stayed the whole time. After suffering the indecency of being searched I was led into the familiar visiting room I'd hoped to never see again. Memories of times spent with Zay swirled in my mind and when I looked at the bathroom door my pussy spasmed with wetness. But just as quick I thought about all the pussy he probably got from hoes working here, and that stopped the throbbing between my legs instantly. Sometimes I felt like such a fool.

It seemed like it took forever for Rocko to get to the visiting room, but after fifteen minutes I saw him breeze through the door. If it wasn't for his face he could've been a stranger, because his hair was long and braided, and he'd definitely found a push up routine that worked.

"Damn, bruh, you serious about the workout, ain't you?" I asked, opening my arms wide and stepping into his welcoming embrace.

"Ain't shit else to do, and Ima make this life sentence last as long as possible."

"I'm glad you're out the hole so I can actually touch you. I swear you have no idea how much I've missed you," I said, fighting against the tears that wanted to spring forth.

"I missed you too, and you better not start crying up in here, because if you make me cry it'll ruin my prison cred."

"Nigga, you ain't got no prison cred yet, you just got here," I replied, laughing and sitting in the chair next to his.

"Shit, you ain't see the nigga I smashed. Big dude thought he weighed in and could pick on the new kid, but he found out quick what the rock in Rocko stood for."

"You gotta chill, bruh, I don't want you getting into trouble…"

"What are they gonna do to me, Carmen, give me more time?" he asked sarcastically.

I knew he was right, and what I was really worried about was him getting hurt or killed, but I knew I couldn't tell him how to do his time. It was his bid and I couldn't do it for him, but I'd do it with him.

"You want something from the machines?" I asked, pulling money out of my sweat pants pocket.

"Sit right here for a sec," he said, getting up and going over to the CO. I watched as they exchanged a few words and then Rocko was headed back towards our table.

"Sit right here and I'll get the food," he said, taking the money from my hand and going to the machine.

I started to object because he wasn't allowed to handle the money or cross the yellow line where the snack machines were located, but it was obvious he knew what he was doing. I did as I was told, casually looking around at what was quickly becoming a familiar environment to me. It was hard to see Rocko like this and inside my heart ached for what he was about to go through, but I had to keep my brave face on for him. A few minutes later he returned with a couple turkey subs, two Sprites, hot pork rinds for me, and sour cream chips for him.

"Maybe you do have some prison cred," I said, smiling.

"I do what I can do. So, how're my son and niece doing?" suddenly serious, his face becoming a mask I couldn't see behind.

"They're good, they actually get along like brother and sister. RJ misses you though," I informed him with a heavy heart.

I could see the raw pain in his eyes and it hurt me because I didn't know how to take it away. The only insurances I could give were that his son was safe and loved. Thankfully, the people who had taken him were kind to him, and Zay had done his part by getting him back without incident. The experience itself was still traumatic, because in the blink of an eye RJ had become somewhat of an orphan.

"I miss him too. When are you bringing him to see me?"

"I wanted to make sure that's what you wanted before I did that."

"I need to see him. I need to look in his eyes and know that what happened to him won't have lasting effects," he said.

"I don't think it will. I mean the first few weeks he was quiet and withdrawn, but once I started showing him pictures of me and you he started to trust me. I'm not sure he understands the concept of family, but he knows he's safe with us," I said.

"Is he safe though?"

"What's that supposed to mean?" I asked cautiously, opening my soda and taking a drink.

"You know exactly what I'm asking you, Carmen. Is my son safe around your husband?"

"Why would you even think some shit like that? You know Zayvion would never hurt a kid," I replied, annoyed that we were having this conversation.

"I'm gonna tell you again, and for the last time, we don't know Zavion. You've seen the *Godfather* enough to know that little boys become grown men, and they want revenge for shit that has happened. Honestly, I'm surprised we got RJ back alive, but that was probably because Zay knew you'd go after the connect if he didn't ensure that RJ was returned."

"So then why would you think he'd turn around and hurt RJ now?" I asked.

"Because he knows at some point my son is gonna come for him, once he knows the truth."

"So, basically you're telling me that you're gonna send the little boy I'm raising for you to kill my own kid's father?" I asked, wondering if he was really hearing himself.

"What I'm telling you is that my son is gonna want the truth of why his dad is serving a life sentence. Do I not owe him the truth?"

It was impossible for me to say no to that question, but if I said yes then I was basically signing my own husband's death warrant.

"So, I guess this is about you being innocent of these charges, according to you?" I asked.

"I can tell by just the way you say that, that you're starting to question if your husband had been truthful with you. I guess beyond the pain of your initial doubt of my word I should feel happy that you're even considering I might be telling the truth."

"Rocko, I..."

"Carmen, I'm your brother, and while I've made some fucked up decisions I came completely clean with you six months ago. I told you my ugly truths, yet I still see doubt in your eyes, little sister. Let's see if knowing more truth will help you," he said, taking a piece of paper from his pocket and sliding it across the table to me, I took it and opened it to find a Richmond, Virginia address.

I looked back up at him for some explanation, but I couldn't read the look in his eyes.

"What's this?" I asked.

"That's Iesha's address. She no longer works here, but I managed to find out where she lives."

"Okay, and why would I need this information?" I asked, still puzzled.

"I thought you might go see her and have a much-needed conversation. Especially since she just had a baby two weeks ago."

His words hit me like the force of a chopper bullet and left me utterly speechless. All I could do is stare at him.

Initially my mind went blank. Then I was studying Rocko for any hint that he was lying, or at least that his implication was bullshit. In my heart, I believed that Zayvion was probably getting some pussy on the side, but there's no way the nigga was stupid enough to get another bitch pregnant.

"It's not his baby," I said, in a dazed tone.

"It's not? Well, I can tell you first hand that they don't sell condoms on commissary, but that don't stop a nigga from getting his nut."

"It's not his baby," I repeated, my voice sounding weaker to my own ears than the first time.

"I won't argue with you, Carmen. If it's not his baby, then your pop up visit won't matter too much."

"This ain't Iesha's address, I know where she lives because…"

"He got her a house," Rocko said calmly.

"Oh…oh God, what do I do? I can accept a lot of things, but not this," I said, shaking my head. The instant pain in my gut forced my hands to my stomach as I tried to figure out if I was gonna be sick or if my baby was in danger. There were no words for the emotions I was feeling except complete and utter disbelief. And swiftly building rage.

"After you hear my plan you'll forgive him, but on your terms."

Chapter 17
Rocko

After I laid out what I had in mind for Zayvion, I changed the subject and made small talk for the rest of my visit. I knew I needed to give Carmen time to process everything, because she couldn't and wouldn't make a decision until she could see clearly. I hadn't seen it clearly until I'd found out this piece of information, but when I did I realized the clock could be reset and the playing field leveled. Of course, everything came with a risk, and this was a huge one, because I'd never forgive myself if I put my sister in harm's way. I just had to believe that everything I'd learned since all this bullshit began would allow me to see clearer and move with more calculation.

After my visit, I made the walk back to my floor with my mind a few hundred miles away. While I may have understood that my greed played a part in how shit unfolded, I still couldn't overlook the fact that the nigga I'd bled with had set me up. True enough, I'd broken cardinal rule #1 and I'd told on him, but I'd done it because I had to. He'd set me up because he wanted to, because in the end when the smoke cleared he wanted it all to himself. It was time he learned that you couldn't take your eyes off the board just because you thought it was checkmate. When you had your opponent cornered you damn well better make sure there was no way out, because it wasn't no fun when the rabbit had the gun.

"You got your pass?" CO Hardy asked once I reached my floor.

I handed it to him through the bars and he slid the gate open. I'd been hoping his pudgy ass wouldn't come into work today because I needed to handle business, but I got no such luck. It didn't take long to identify the good cops from bad cops in prison, even though that was a crazy statement, because a cop was a cop, which meant they couldn't be trusted. The problem with Hardy was that he was a 5'10, balding, chubby guy, who thought he was one of the cool kids in school. Not exactly a redneck, but he had hillbilly tendencies, and for some reason he thought a mufucka wouldn't get on his ass and ride him rough.

Some COs came in for a paycheck, while others wanted that sense of authority for all those years they never got to spend their lunch money because it was confiscated. And then you had those ambitious mufuckas who wanted to rise through the ranks until they became warden. They made big shit out of the small shit, and the actual big shit damn near ended up on the 10 o'clock news! That was CO Hardy.

I really didn't need his brand of bullshit today, so I didn't even make eye contact as I came on the floor. More than likely I'd still end up getting shook down before his shift ended because I'd gone to visitation. I was almost starting to believe he just didn't like black people, but I didn't go there just yet because every white man didn't think like that.

Instead, of going and getting my cellphone out of its hiding place I hopped on the prison phone and dialed the number I had memorized. It took about 5 minutes to get through all the automated bullshit, but finally I heard the sweet sound of her voice.

"Hey, baby, what's up?" I asked, smiling.

"Not a whole lot, just hoping you would call. I actually just woke up from my nap."

"Oh yeah. Lazy ass," I said, teasing her.

"Hey, you better be nice to me or I'll kick your ass, and you know I could."

"Yeah, and only because I wouldn't fight back. You know I love you too much for all that."

"Yeah, I know, and I love you too," she replied.

"I know you do, you've proven that. I would've called you earlier, but I got a surprise visit from my sister."

"Oh yeah? How did that go?"

"It was good, you know how much I've missed her and RJ. She didn't bring him, but she said he's doing good and he seems to be okay after everything that happened."

"That's definitely good news. I'm glad he's okay after something so traumatic, especially since he lost his mom too."

"I don't ever want him to forget her because she was my friend and always there when I needed her, but I think my sister will do a good job raising him until..."

"So, I take it you had that conversation?" she asked, hesitantly.

"Yeah, we did, but it went better than I thought it would. I think she's finally starting to believe I'm innocent."

"'Bout time! Shit, the dick can't be that good to have her disillusioned," she stated with conviction.

"Really? So, I guess you'd believe bad things about me easily, huh?"

"No, baby, because your dick *is* that good," she replied, laughing.

She made me laugh too, which was one of the reasons I loved her, because it wasn't easy to laugh anymore or find a reason to be happy. She gave me that reason and the hope needed to get out of bed in the morning. A lot of females would've talked a good game up until that gavel fell and they would've run because a life sentence ain't no bitch, especially when it can't be beat. Abby wasn't like most women, which was definitely a surprise considering she was 24, beautiful, and had her whole life in front of her. All she wanted was me though.

"So, how are you feeling?" I asked.

"I'm fine, babe, you worry too much. And you wonder why I was hesitant to tell you about me getting sick."

"You better have told me or I'd kick your ass, and you already know that I'm gonna worry about you no matter what."

"I promise you I'll take care of myself and your little girl inside me, okay!" she said.

"I know you will, and I trust you, baby. I want you to get something to eat, because I know you got shit to do and I'll talk to you tonight."

"Alright. Please stay out of trouble, because I don't want you to go back to the hole."

"Everything is fine, babe, don't stress. I love you," I said.

"I love you too."

I hung up the phone with a smile on my face, feeling hope swell inside me in a way it never had before. In the streets, I focused on money and business, not love, but it was times like this when you realized what's important. I went to my cell and found my cellmate sleeping, so I decided to walk a few laps around the unit and think about everything that had to happen for shit to change. I'd never doubted Carmen before, but I knew what I'd outlined for her would be incredibly difficult.

Any ordinary female wouldn't have been up to the task, but my little sister was cut from a different cloth.

Knowing that allowed me to breathe easier. I'd just made my second trip past the backdoor when I heard someone whisper my name. The building I was housed in had three floors that were connected by front and back stairwells. I lived on the first floor, which meant anyone going to the chow hall had to come past my backdoor. If the right shift was on most mufuckas could kick it or conduct business in the hallway.

Today wasn't the right shift, but if I stood facing the window I could have a conversation without Hardy knowing. Quickly, I made another lap and stopped at the window closest to the door.

"What's up?" I asked.

"I came through earlier, but I heard you were in visitation."

"Yeah, my sister came to see me. What did you need though?" I asked, casually checking my surroundings to make sure no one was in hearing distance.

"I just got a little green for you."

There was nothing I could do about the numerous eyes of the other inmates, because somebody always saw something. But when I turned around to survey the unit I did so looking for CO Hardy. When I saw another inmate had his attention at the booth I quickly stepped to the doorway, and took the half full Ziploc bag offered to me, tucking it into my boxers before resuming my spot at the window.

"What's this cost?" I asked.

"Just a little something to welcome you out of the hole. It don't cost you nothing."

"Ain't nothing free, especially not behind these walls. Kick it to me straight. What do you want, Ham?" I asked, turning away from the window to look him square in the eyes.

"I wanna know how my cousin got from under those indictments that damn quick, and how you end up in here on a 5-year-old cold case?"

Two things you could always count on in prison was somebody trying the new kid, and somebody researching the new kid. It didn't surprise me that Ham had asked around about me, despite the fact that we'd both heard of each other. What did surprise me were his questions about Zay, because thus far he was the only mufucka I knew that had picked up on the fact that something wasn't right. The problem was, opening my mouth did me more harm than good.

"I fuck with you, Hambone, and I know you're block tested and hood approved, but you're gonna have to talk to your cousin about that."

"You know how that conversation is gonna go, because if something ain't right he damn sure can't afford to admit it. I want the truth," he replied.

What he said sounded good, but I knew he didn't want the truth. He wanted leverage. There was nothing to be gained and everything to lose by giving him what he wanted, which made my answer easy.

"I don't know how he beat his case, but if something was funny about it it's gonna come out sooner or later. Until then speculation does neither of us any good, so let's stick to getting this money. Feel me?"

I could tell just by the way he was looking at me that he was searching for some hidden message in my words, but there was none there. I walked away and continued to do my laps around the unit until I saw CO Hardy take his dinner break, and then I went to my cell. This time my cellmate was awake.

"What up, Kayo?" I asked.

"Shit, bruh, caught that quick power nap and now I'm ready to go out here and get this workout in. You wit it?"

"Give me a minute and I'm on my way," I replied, peeling off my red jumpsuit.

I put on some shorts, slid my Airmax on, and followed him out the door, but I didn't go to the back of the unit where we were allowed to workout. Two doors down from my cell was where my white boy Farmer stayed, and I paid him to hold all my contraband. After I dropped the weed off I joined my celli and we got to work. I'd known Kayo before prison because he was from Manassas and we'd gotten a little money together.

It had been a while since those days though, because he was already 10 years in on a 50-year bid. He'd spent most of that time in the county jail fighting through the appeal process. Neither of us would be here long, but it was good to have somebody who was likeminded to pass time with. Everybody thought he was my little brother, even though he was older than me, because we resembled each other, except he was only 5'7. He was stocky and ready to fight at a moment's notice, so when I'd arrived on the scene mufuckas knew we were double the trouble.

We worked out hard for two hours straight doing push-ups, dips, sit-ups, and jumping jacks until I felt like I would fall over. I knew he trained hard because he was 107 Hoover Crip, and he always had to be ready for war, but I was simply trying to keep my mind focused and my anger in check. After the workout I grabbed my shower stuff and hit the rain box, missing my own shower at home and trying to block out the memories of Kat and I at times like this. I was with Abby and fully committed to her, but I missed Kat sometimes and I didn't see anything wrong with that.

Every time I looked at my son I'd see her, and the same was probably true for Abby and our daughter. When she'd first told me, she was pregnant I'd almost lost my mind because I didn't know whether she should have it or have an abortion. It wasn't that I didn't want our baby, but I did feel guilty about making her a lifetime single mom, because that wasn't fair. When we'd started having sex on the regular she'd gone on the pill, but we'd been too little too late, and abortion wasn't in her vocabulary. I was thankful for that and her loyalty and I vowed to give her everything I never gave Kat.

"Vargas!" someone called from the shower door.

"Yeah?"

"You need to go to medical."

Grabbing my towel, I quickly dried off and went to my cell to get dressed. Even though I smelled like Irish Spring soap I still took the time to handle my hygiene before putting on a fresh jumpsuit and my shoes, and heading for the control booth.

"Straight to medical, Vargas, no detours," CO Hardy said, handing me my pass.

I didn't even bother acknowledging his attempt at micro-managing, I just took the pass and waited for the gate to swing open. I knew why I was going to medical, so I didn't need nobody to tell me to go straight there. When I walked into the medical area there were two other inmates waiting, but I spotted her immediately and she waved me into the back office.

"How are you doing today, Mr. Vargas?" she asked before closing the door.

"I'm good now," I replied, pulling her into my arms and kissing her thoroughly.

"Mmm, I'd ask you if you missed me, but that's apparent."

"Of course, I missed you, baby, every moment that we're apart. How much time so we have together?" I asked, placing kisses all over her neck.

"I can keep you for at least an hour. I gave the doctor $1,000 to sign an order for blood work, a physical, and a urine sample."

"Sounds like fun, but I've got other things in mind," I informed her, pushing her pants and panties down before lifting her up onto the exam table.

"Oh really? Am I going to like these things?"

"No, my sweet Abby, you're gonna love them. And soon I'll be home to do them to you."

Chapter 18
Zay
3 days later…

"Are you staying again tonight?"

"Stop talking," I replied, pushing Dara's head back into my lap, my dick sliding smoothly between her lips.

I wrapped my hand up in her hair to prevent her from taking it all the way out again, and to make sure that every time she went down I hit that little thing hanging in the back of her throat like it was a speed bag. The way her mouth was always wet no matter how long she sucked dick, and her techniques, plus the lack of gag reflex would make you fall in love with her. To her credit though she'd warned me before we ever got this far, when I was still trying to put her on the team.

"Oh-oh shit," I mumbled, right before I came deep in her throat.

Of course, she swallowed every drop and continued sucking because I was still hard in her jaws, but I'd gotten what I needed and now it was time to go.

"Baby, I'm good," I said, releasing the hold I had on her hair.

"I'm not," she replied, quickly climbing on top of me and straddling me.

"Dara, I don't have time right now, I gotta…"

"My pussy is good enough for you to make time," she said, grabbing my dick and guiding it inside her warm wetness.

I opened my mouth to protest, but she put her hand over my mouth and began riding at a full gallop. Out of all the women I had in rotation she was the most assertive, and sometimes forceful, but I liked that shit. Her eyes blazed down at me with an insatiable hunger as her platinum blond hair swung in rhythm to her fierce ride. This was what I called taking the dick.

"Dara…Dara…I…"

"Stop talking!" she growled, moving faster and pumping harder.

In the mirror above the bed I could see her juicy ass waving and that turned me on even more.

"Choke me."

"What?" I asked, confused.

"Choke me!" she screamed, smacking me across the face hard.

Immediately my hands went to her neck and squeezed and within two downward thrusts her eyes lost focus and she came like a tropical storm. I felt my own nit coming, but suddenly she stopped and pulled my hands from around her neck.

"Wh-what are you doing?" I asked.

"Oh, I'm good now," she replied, hopping up off me and going into the bathroom.

"You're…you're good? Okay, I'm glad, but you need to come finish what you started," I said, frustrated.

Her response was to close the bathroom door, leaving me with only the memory of her 42 DD's bouncing in the afternoon sunlight, and a hard dick that was far from satisfied. When I heard the shower come on I thought that was my invitation, and I was out of the bed and at the door quick, only to find it locked.

"Oh, she with the bullshit," I said to myself, picking up my clothes off the floor and getting dressed.

By the time, she finished her shower I was sitting at the foot of her bed, waiting to verbally blow her shit back.

"So, we gonna play games now?" I asked, when she came out of the bathroom naked, water glistening on her body in a way that had my dick knocking at the zipper to my jeans.

"I'm not playing games, Zayvion. I was trying to ask if you were staying here tonight because I have a late scheduled appointment to do, but you were more interested in cumming down my throat. You got yours and I got mine, it's all good."

"You know I wanted to get mine inside you," I said, watching her naked ass sway as she went into her closet to get dressed.

"You got enough mouths to feed without putting a baby in me. Besides, I've got two of my own and I ain't ready for a third."

"You're an OB/GYN and you deliver babies all day, so I know you love kids. Plus, you're a great mom..."

"Why does it sound like you're trying to convince me to have your baby? I'll be delivering your wife's baby in a couple weeks, and you just had one a couple weeks ago, so where in your mind is it a good idea for us to do some irresponsible shit like have a kid?" she asked, annoyed.

I didn't even know how in the hell we ended up having this conversation, because I definitely didn't need to have any more kids outside of my marriage. Carmen already had me wearing condoms now, and I was getting the feeling that it was more about her suspecting me of cheating than practice for after our baby was born. Plus, this thing with Dara and I was casual, just some fuck buddy type shit that had started when I had to find a new doctor for Carmen. It had taken some fast talking and serious pipe laying to get Dara to be her doctor, but she was the best around. And the sex was righteous too.

"You're right. I'm trippin', to answer your earlier question, I don't know if I'm coming back tonight because I gotta ride to Richmond and check on my baby and baby mama. She ain't been answering my calls or text," I said.

"You should probably go check on Carmen too, because you being here for the last few days means y'all beefin' 'bout something. She doesn't need to be that stressed this late in her pregnancy."

I started to say some smart shit about the concerned doctor who was fucking her patient's husband, but I let that go.

"What time will you be home?" I asked when she came out of the closet.

"I don't know, but if you wanna finish what we started just come over," she replied, taking my face in her hands and kissing me with enough passion to have me pulling at her scrub pants, trying to get them off.

"I said tonight," she said, laughing and swatting my hands away.

From past experience, I knew that she knew how to make a mufucka beg, but I wasn't gonna do that right now. Standing up I pulled her into my arms and kissed her one more time before letting her go, and making my way downstairs to the living room. Dara may have been a single mother of two, but she provided well for them because the split-level 4 bedroom, 3.5 bath house she had in Springfield, Virginia didn't come cheap.

Women who were about their money were always sexy to me. As I grabbed my phone off the coffee table and headed for the front door I gave serious thought to coming back tonight. Her kids would be back from camp soon, which meant all these overnight visits would stop.

Plus, it allowed me not to have to deal with Carmen, but I was still close enough that I could be there when she sent the call that the baby was coming.

Normally, I'd try to work out our differences because I didn't like to argue, but I didn't even know why we were beefing! Ever since she'd come back from her visit with that nigga Rocko she'd been distant. I mean we still fucked, but I think that was because she wanted it, and it had nothing to do with me. I knew she was always gonna feel some type of way about him being in prison for life, so I guess I just had to give her time and space.

Normally, she would've been blowing my phone up if I'd spent two nights away from home, but looking at my phone now I saw my only missed call came from Burnette. Sliding behind the wheel of my car I was unsure of my destination, so I called Burnette to see what she had on her mind.

"Where are you?" she asked, answering on the second ring.

"I'm out and about. Why? What's going on?"

"Nothing much, I've just been wanting to see you. When do you think that'll be possible?"

"Is that your way of saying you miss me?" I asked, laughing.

"Something like that, but don't let it go to your head, sweetheart. Are you coming to see me or what?"

"Yeah, I'll be at your door in a little while, but I gotta handle something first."

"Hurry, I've had this vibrator in me for about an hour and my sheets are soaked with my juices," she purred, hanging up before I could get a word in.

I cranked the engine and pointed the car in the direction of my house, wanting to check on Carmen and the kids before heading to Richmond. Maybe it would be some type of peace offering to pick them up some of their favorite fast food. I was halfway home when my phone rang and I saw that it was Carmen calling.

"I was just thinking about you," I said as soon as I answered.

"I bet you were. Where are you?"

"I'm on my way home, but Ima stop at Popeye's first. What do you want to eat?" I asked.

"Are you going to the Popeye's not far from the house? Because they have the best fries."

"Yes, baby, that's where I'm going. Do you want anything besides fries?"

"Nope, I'll be good with that. How long before you get here?" she asked.

"About 30 minutes."

"See you later," she replied disconnecting the call.

I'd expected a much chillier conversation considering how much time I'd spent away from home, but I was glad we weren't clashing. Carmen was still my #1 at the end of the day, no matter what we went through or who I was fucking on the side. She was that bottom bitch that held my life together, which was one of the reasons I hated fighting with her. Sadly, I knew we had more fighting ahead of us because at some point I was gonna have to be real about Iesha and our son, Xavier.

I wanted all my kids to know each other and grow up together, but that would be a lot to ask of Carmen, especially with the whole Rocko situation still being so fresh. The moment I pulled into the Popeye's parking lot the smell of that good chicken had my mouth watering, but the sight of the red and blue flashing lights behind me dried it up quick. I wasn't nervous because I didn't have shit on me or in the car, but any nigga who had ever dealt with the police before knew it was natural to be leery. Pulling into a parking space I brought the car to a stop and waited.

"Driver, shut off your engine, stick your hands out the window, open the door and step out," came the commands over the cop car's loudspeaker.

Immediately my stomach started bubbling, because this wasn't no routine traffic stop. I did as I was told, slow and steady.

"Now walk backwards to the sound of my voice," I was told.

I'd only taken about 5 steps before I was grabbed up and handcuffed before I could get a word out.

"What did I do, officer?" I asked as calmly as I could.

"We'll tell you in just a minute, Mr. Miller, we got one little thing to get out of the way."

While one cop searched my car, I was patted down and then led to a cop car where I was roughly shoved in the backseat. At first, I'd thought there'd only been one cop car behind me, but now I saw that the parking lot was aglow with lights from at least six police cruisers. This definitely wasn't no random stop or traffic violation. Suddenly, my door was opened and a tall, young, clean cut white guy in a navy blue suit identified himself as Detective Cala, and read me my rights.

I opened my mouth to ask him what the fuck was going on, but he shut the door and told me he'd see me at the police station. They didn't make me wait either, because a cop jumped in the driver's seat and we were on the move.

"Yo, why am I being arrested?" I asked.

"I'm not allowed to answer any of your questions, sir."

"You gotta tell me what the fuck you locking me up for!" I exclaimed angrily.

Of course, I didn't even get a response this time, which pissed me off even more. Snapping on this cop wasn't gonna get me out any faster, so the best thing I could do for myself was to sit back and chill, and call my lawyer a.s.a.p. The ride to the station took an uneventful fifteen minutes, which gave me the necessary time to compose myself so I could think clearly versus emotionally.

Loudon County police station was small, kind of like a mom and pop operation of the judicial system, so it didn't surprise me when I was pulled out of the car, brought inside, and stuck in a room the size of my old prison cell. I tried to ask for my lawyer call, but the cop just walked out the room and closed the door behind him. It was a long 30 minutes before the door opened again, and in walked the same detective that had read me my rights.

"Are you gonna explain why I'm here?" I asked calmly.

"Sure, we can talk about that, Mr. Miller. As you know your rights have been read to you and you can stop this conversation at any time if you wanna speak to your lawyer."

"Okay. So why am I here?" I asked again.

"Do you know an Iesha Hayes?'

With just that one question my stomach dropped to my feet. If a Northern Virginia cop was asking me about my baby mama all the way in Richmond then it wasn't good.

"She's my son's mother. Why, what happened?"

"And when was the last time you saw her?"

"I don't know. What the fuck happened?" I asked again, becoming more agitated by the minute.

"Would you say you two had a good relationship or were there issues?"

"I'm not answering a goddamn question until you tell me what all this has to do with Iesha," I stated.

"I think you know what this has to do with Iesha, since you killed her. I'm not judging you because crimes of passion…"

"Lawyer," I said, reeling from what I'd just heard, but still having the presence of mind to know that talking did me absolutely no good.

"Lawyer?"

"I ain't got shit to say without my lawyer," I replied, hoping the sour taste in my mouth didn't turn into vomit right here and now.

"Well, that's you're right, sir. I gotta be honest though, the best lawyer in the world won't get you out of this one," he said, opening the door and leaving me to deal with the millions of thoughts racing through my brain.

If Iesha was dead, where the fuck was my son? How could they think I killed my newborn son's mom? This shit was fucking crazy and it definitely felt like a set up. But who would…

"Miller, you've got five minutes," a cop said, opening the door right before Carmen walked in.

"Oh God, babe, I'm so glad you're here," I said, breathing a sigh of relief as she sat down across from me at the small wooden table.

"Sweetheart, there's nowhere else I'd be."

"Listen, babe, this shit is a mistake and I'm being set up, but before I get into all that I've gotta tell you about Iesha and…"

"And Xavier," she said, finishing my sentence for me.

It wasn't until she spoke my son's name that some of the fog began to clear a little. Carmen had somewhat of a smile on her face, but her eyes didn't match the smile. Her eyes swirled with determination and…rage.

"So, you know?" I asked.

"I only found out recently, from Rocko of all people."

"Rocko? How the fuck…"

"Don't tell me you've underestimated the resourceful-ness of my brother? A man with a life sentence has noth-ing to do except to think, because the mind is a terrible thing to waste," she said seriously.

"He…he did this? He killed…"

"How could he kill anyone, sweetheart? Aside from the President of the United States he's probably got the most ironclad alibi. What about you?" she asked, sweetly.

"Wh-what?"

"Where have you been for the last few days, Zayvion, because it's just not like you to not come home to your wife and kids."

I opened my mouth to tell her exactly where the hell I'd been, but a little voice in my head told me it didn't matter. This was bigger than who I was fucking.

"What is this?" I asked, studying my wife as carefully as I would any opponent.

"I know that look in your eyes, Zayvion. You're try-ing to put the pieces together, huh? Well, first let me put your mind at ease," she said, leaning across the table as if to tell me secrets.

"Xavier is safe, and he's at home with his sister and cousin. Iesha was killed with your gun, that has your fingerprints on it, and your semen was found inside her. Oh, and it looks like force, so that means an aggravated rape on top of first-degree murder. I think that covers everything."

"Wh-why would you do this? Why would you take me away from my children?" I asked, weakly, seeing my life and everything I knew vanish before my eyes. I always knew that karma was real and that bitch came for everyone but I didn't expect to be married to her. The thin line between love and hate had been erased and now I understood what side Carmen was on, but I still couldn't believe it.

"Because I know you've always got a plan and a way out. Fair exchange ain't never robbery."

To be continued…
A Hustler's Deceit 3
Coming Soon

Stay Connected with Us!

Text **LOCKDOWN** to 22828 to stay up-to-date with new releases, sneak peaks, contests and more…

Thank you!

Coming Soon from Lock Down Publications/Ca$h Presents

BOW DOWN TO MY GANGSTA

By **Ca$h & Jamaica**

TORN BETWEEN TWO

By **Coffee**

BLOOD OF A BOSS **IV**

By **Askari**

BRIDE OF A HUSTLA **III**

THE FETTI GIRLS

By **Destiny Skai**

WHEN A GOOD GIRL GOES BAD **II**

By **Adrienne**

LOVE & CHASIN' PAPER **II**

By **Qay Crockett**

THE HEART OF A GANGSTA **II**

By **Jerry Jackson**

TO DIE IN VAIN **II**

By **ASAD**

LOYAL TO THE GAME **II**

By **TJ & Jelissa**

A DOPEBOY'S PRAYER **II**
By **Eddie "Wolf" Lee**
A HUSTLER'S DECEIT **III**
THE BOSS MAN'S DAUGHTERS **III**
BAE BELONGS TO ME **II**
By **Aryanna**
A KINGPIN'S AMBITON
By **Ambitious**

Available Now
(CLICK TO PURCHASE)
RESTRAINING ORDER **I & II**
By **CA$H & Coffee**
LOVE KNOWS NO BOUNDARIES **I II & III**
By **Coffee**
LAY IT DOWN **I & II**
LAST OF A DYING BREED
By **Jamaica**
LOYAL TO THE GAME
By **TJ & Jelissa**
PUSH IT TO THE LIMIT
By **Bre' Hayes**

BLOOD OF A BOSS **I II & III**

By **Askari**

THE STREETS BLEED MURDER **I, II & III**

THE HEART OF A GANGSTA

By **Jerry Jackson**

CUM FOR ME

CUM FOR ME 2

CUM FOR ME 3

An **LDP Erotica Collaboration**

BRIDE OF A HUSTLA **I & II**

By **Destiny Skai**

WHEN A GOOD GIRL GOES BAD

By **Adrienne**

A GANGSTER'S REVENGE **I II III & IV**

THE BOSS MAN'S DAUGHTERS

THE BOSS MAN'S DAUGHTERS II

A SAVAGE LOVE **I & II**

BAE BELONGS TO ME

By **Aryanna**

A DOPEBOY'S PRAYER

By **Eddie "Wolf" Lee**

WHAT ABOUT US **I & II**

NEVER LOVE AGAIN

THUG ADDICTION

By **Kim Kaye**

THE KING CARTEL **I, II & III**

By **Frank Gresham**

THESE NIGGAS AIN'T LOYAL **I, II & III**

By **Nikki Tee**

GANGSTA SHYT **I II &III**

By **CATO**

THE ULTIMATE BETRAYAL

By **Phoenix**

DON'T FU#K WITH MY HEART **I & II**

By **Linnea**

BOSS'N UP **I & II**

By **Royal Nicole**

I LOVE YOU TO DEATH

By Destiny J

I RIDE FOR MY HITTA

I STILL RIDE FOR MY HITTA

By **Misty Holt**

LOVE & CHASIN' PAPER

By **Qay Crockett**

TO DIE IN VAIN

By **ASAD**

BOOKS BY LDP'S CEO, CA$H
(CLICK TO PURCHASE)

TRUST IN NO MAN

TRUST IN NO MAN 2

TRUST IN NO MAN 3

BONDED BY BLOOD

SHORTY GOT A THUG

THUGS CRY

THUGS CRY 2

THUGS CRY 3

TRUST NO BITCH

TRUST NO BITCH 2

TRUST NO BITCH 3

TIL MY CASKET DROPS

RESTRAINING ORDER

RESTRAINING ORDER 2

IN LOVE WITH A CONVICT

Coming Soon

BONDED BY BLOOD 2

BOW DOWN TO MY GANGSTA

CPSIA information can be obtained
at www.ICGtesting.com
Printed in the USA
LVHW082347030421
683379LV00035B/749